grk
and the
hot dog trail

Joshua Doder

Typeset by FISH Books, Enfield, Middx.
...d in the UK by CPI ...Boo...arque, Croydon, CR...

Andersen Press · London

First published in 2006 by
Andersen Press Limited,
20 Vauxhall Bridge Road, London SW1V 2SA
www.andersenpress.co.uk
Reprinted 2007 (twice), 2008 (twice), 2009

British Library Cataloguing in Publication Data available

ISBN 978 184 270 553 7

Printe   ) 4TD

grk

hot dog trail

Chapter 1

The flight left in an hour. In a few minutes, they would be called to the gate. If he was going to do it, he had to do it now.

Tim stood up. He tugged the lead. Grk struggled to his feet and looked around the departure lounge of JFK International Airport, sniffing the air and wagging his tail.

Tim looked at his mother. 'Mum? I'm going for a pee.'

'Leave Grk here,' said Mrs Malt. 'I'll look after him.'

'Actually, it's not me who needs a pee. It's Grk.'

Mrs Malt nodded. 'Don't be too long. We have to get on the plane in fifteen minutes.'

'I'll be quick,' said Tim.

Together, he and Grk hurried across the departure lounge. At the exit, he glanced back. Through the crowds, he could see his mother sitting on a bench, reading a newspaper. Tim whispered, 'Sorry, Mum.' Of course, she couldn't hear him. But he would have felt even worse if he hadn't said anything.

He showed his passport to the guard, who waved him past. Tim hurried through the airport, following the signs to the taxi rank. Grk trotted alongside him.

There was a short queue for taxis. Tim stood at the back of the queue and waited impatiently, worried that his mother would come searching for him. How long would she wait before she started worrying? Five minutes? Ten? And then what would she do? Would she run round the airport, searching for him? Or would she call the police immediately?

But neither Mrs Malt nor the police had arrived by the time that Tim reached the front of the queue. He opened the door. Grk jumped onto the back seat. Tim clambered after him and slammed the door. 'Good morning,' said the driver. 'Welcome to New York. What's your destination?'

'The Bramley Building, please.'

'Coming right up.'

The taxi accelerated down the sliproad and joined the highway.

The traffic was terrible. It took almost an hour to cross Brooklyn, plunge through the tunnel under the Hudson River and reach Manhattan. The streets of the Upper West Side were even more clogged. Finally, the taxi pulled up outside the Bramley Building. The driver said, 'This is it, kid.'

'Okay,' said Tim.

The driver said, 'You wanna give me a tip, give me a tip. Whatever you can afford. You don't want to give me a tip, you don't have to. It's a free country, right?'

'Thanks,' said Tim. 'I'd like to give you a tip. There's just one problem. I don't have any money.'

The taxi driver laughed. 'You British! You have a great sense of humour.'

'I'm not joking,' said Tim. 'I really don't have any money. Can I take your address? I'll get my mum to send the money tomorrow.'

The taxi driver laughed even louder. 'Irony, right? I love it. You are so ironic.'

'I'm not being ironic,' said Tim. 'I really don't have any money.'

Immediately, the taxi driver stopped laughing. He whirled round and poked his head through the sliding glass windows that divided the front seats from the back seats. 'Forget the tip. You don't wanna pay me a tip, don't pay me no tip. But just pay the fare, okay? Pay the fare.'

'I don't have any money.'

'Enough with your irony already,' said the taxi driver. 'Just give me the money.'

Tim shook his head and spoke very slowly. 'I do not have any money.'

'Right! We're going to the police!' The driver thrust his foot down on the accelerator, revving the engine.

'No, no,' said Tim. If they went to the police, he would be sent back to his parents. Then he couldn't do anything. He wouldn't be able to help anyone. 'We don't have to go anywhere near the police.'

'That's fine by me,' said the driver. 'But where's my money?'

Tim thought quickly. He pointed at the Bramley Building. 'My parents are in there. I'll go inside, get some money and come back down.'

The taxi driver shook his head. 'Kid, do you think I was born yesterday?'

'No,' said Tim. 'I think you were probably born about forty years ago.'

'Forty-three,' said the taxi driver. 'I've driven cabs for seven. And I've learnt one thing. If a guy says he'll go inside and bring back the fare, he never comes back.'

Tim thrust his hands into his pockets. He found a piece of chewing gum, two doggie treats, some string, lots of fluff and his passport. 'You could keep this.' He offered the passport to the taxi driver. 'Till I come back with the money.'

'What's that?'

'My passport.'

The taxi driver shook his head. 'Worth nothing to me, kid. I'm not touching that.'

Tim frantically tried to think. What could he do? He had no money, and no way of getting money. Then he had an idea. 'I'll leave Grk,' he said.

'Grk? What's Grk?'

'This is Grk,' said Tim. He pointed at the small dog lying on the seat beside him. 'I'll leave him with you. If I leave my dog, I'll definitely come back, won't I?'

The taxi driver stared at Grk.

Grk stared back.

Finally, the taxi driver sighed and nodded. 'Go on, then.'

'Thanks,' said Tim. He jumped out of the taxi before the driver could change his mind.

As Tim walked from the taxi to the Bramley Building, Grk stood up on the seat and stared through the taxi's window, watching Tim with an expression of disbelief.

4

This cannot be happening, Grk's expression seemed to be saying. This cannot be happening!

But it was.

'Hello, little doggy,' said the taxi driver.

Grk turned his head and stared at the taxi driver.

'Shall we be friends?' The taxi driver smiled. He stretched out his right hand to pat Grk's head.

Grk growled and showed his sharp, pointy teeth.

'Okay, okay,' said the taxi driver, withdrawing his hand as fast as he could. 'Let's not be friends.'

As Tim approached the entrance of the Bramley Building, the door was opened by a doorman wearing a long black coat with bright silver buttons.

'Good morning,' said the doorman in a deep voice. 'Welcome to the Bramley Building.'

'Thanks,' said Tim, and walked through the door.

'My name is Roderick,' said the doorman. 'How can I help you today?'

'I've come to see someone,'said Tim, not stopping, not even slowing down, just heading straight for the lifts.

'Hey! Who have you come to see?'

Tim didn't reply or stop. He just kept walking towards the lifts.

'Come back!' The doorman was furious. 'You can't just walk in here! I'm the doorman, right? Y'understand? You have to tell me who you've come to see!'

Beside the lifts, Tim pressed the button marked with an arrow pointing upwards. The door slid open. Tim stepped inside.

For a moment, the doorman considered running after him, or pulling the switch that halted the lifts, or even calling the police. Then he decided that there wasn't much point. That kid looked about ten. Twelve at the most. How much damage could be done by a twelve-year-old kid?

The doorman retreated behind his desk, picked up his copy of the *National Enquirer*, and continued reading about the pink-haired aliens who had recently landed in Tennessee.

Inside the lift, Tim pressed the button marked 15.

The door slid shut. The lift shuddered upwards.

Tim wondered what he would find in the King and Queen's apartment. And, even more importantly, he tried to imagine what he should be looking for. If he saw a clue, would he even know it was a clue?

He thought about Grk, sitting in the back of the taxi. If Tim couldn't find enough money to pay the fare, what would happen? Would Grk belong to the driver? Or would they both be taken to the police station?

He thought about Max and Natascha Raffifi, who were currently awaiting further questions from the New York Police Department. He thought about his father, who would be pacing up and down the hotel room, anxious and impatient. He thought about his mother, who would be running round JFK International Airport, searching for him. Finally, he thought about himself.

Twenty-four hours ago, he had been a normal twelve-year-old boy, visiting New York for the first time, taking a holiday with his parents, his best friends and his dog.

Now, he was a fugitive, a runaway, a liar and, most importantly, a detective.

The lift eased to a standstill. The door slid open.

This is it, thought Tim. There is only one person in the world who is going to discover who really stole the Golden Dachshund. And that person is me.

Tim stepped out onto the fifteenth floor and walked slowly towards apartment 153.

Chapter 2

Two days earlier, things had been so different.

In the afternoon, a Boeing 747 had eased out of the blue sky and roared along the Atlantic coast of the USA. It flew down the length of Long Island, landed at JFK and disgorged two hundred and twenty-one passengers.

Among those two hundred and twenty-one people, there was a doctor, a dentist, a thief, a priest, a lunatic, a fashion model, two rappers, three chefs, six soldiers, seven bankers and twelve members of a basketball team. Five of the passengers wore false teeth. Two had been born at sea and nine were millionaires.

But we are not interested in any of them. We can let them walk through the corridors of JFK, show their passports, collect their bags, meet their relatives or their friends or their drivers, and continue with their own lives.

We are only interested in six of the passengers on that 747. Two adults, three children and one dog. Their names were Mr Malt, Mrs Malt, Timothy Malt, Max Raffifi, Natascha Raffifi and Grk.

It was half term in England, so the Malts, the Raffifis and Grk had come to New York for a short holiday. They were planning to climb the Empire State Building, ride the Staten Island Ferry, shop at Saks Fifth Avenue and see the Golden Dachshund in the new exhibition of Slavic Art at the National Museum.

On the first day, everything went according to plan.

Mr Malt had booked two rooms at the Millard Fillmore Inn, on the corner of 49th Street and Eighth Avenue. Mr and Mrs Malt had one room. Max, Natascha, Tim and Grk shared another. Arriving at the hotel, they all dumped their bags in their rooms, took showers and changed their clothes, then headed out to wander through the streets of New York. They walked around Times Square for an hour, ate sloppy pizza in a noisy restaurant and went to bed early.

The second day started with a huge breakfast of waffles and pancakes and bacon and maple syrup, washed down with never-ending streams of coffee and orange juice.

Grk wasn't allowed inside the café where they ate breakfast. He sat on the pavement, watching them through the window with a plaintive expression. Tim and Natascha took turns to sneak outside with scraps of bacon and pieces of pancake.

After breakfast, they stumbled out of the café, so full that they could hardly breathe. Mr Malt unfolded a map and stared at the street signs, trying to orientate himself. 'Ah-hah,' he said. 'I know exactly where we are. Come on, follow me. This way!'

Mr Malt hurried down the street. Slowly, the others followed him. Tim and Grk came last. Tim clutched his stomach, wishing he hadn't eaten so many waffles. Grk kept sniffing the pavement, hoping he might discover another slice of crispy bacon or a pool of maple syrup.

'Come on, come on,' cried Mr Malt, waving his map. 'This way. No time to waste.' He hurried them from block to block, pointing out landmarks and reading snippets of information from the guidebook. 'That's the Rockefeller Centre,' he said, pointing at a tall graceful tower. 'Built in the 1930s by John D. Rockefeller Junior.' He peered at his map. 'If we go down here, we'll find the Museum of Modern Art. Quick, quick. No dawdling.'

He led them into MOMA – as the Museum of Modern Art is always called – and they sped through the galleries, parading past the Picassos, skipping by the Hoppers, glancing at the Van Goghs and finally coming to a standstill opposite a big brash picture of Marilyn Monroe. 'That's by Andy Warhol,' said Mr Malt. 'He was one of the first Pop Artists.'

Tim, Max and Natascha stared at the picture. Natascha reached into her rucksack, pulled out her notebook and was just about to jot down some notes when Mr Malt said, 'Come on, let's go. Lots more to see. Quick, quick.'

The rest of the day passed in a blur. They ate kebabs in a Greek restaurant, bought socks in Macy's, watched old men playing chess in Bryant Park, rode the ferry to Staten Island, saw the Statue of Liberty, and rode the ferry back again.

That night, they went to the grand opening of the new Slavic Art exhibition at the National Museum.

Chapter 3

The Director of the National Museum clapped his hands together and called for silence. 'Thank you,' he said, speaking into a microphone so everyone could hear him. 'Thank you very much. I should just like to say a few words and then you can go back to drinking this exquisite champagne.'

The room was packed with three hundred people in slick suits and fancy frocks. Waiters walked through the crowd, carrying trays laden with glasses of bubbling champagne and tasty little snacks.

It was the opening night of a new art exhibition. A hundred paintings hung on the walls. Twenty sculptures stood on plinths. In the centre of the room, there was a tall glass case which contained the most important work in the whole exhibition.

A dachshund.

The dachshund didn't yap or snuffle. Nor did it bark, blink or breathe. It stayed absolutely still, standing on its four legs, staring straight ahead.

The Director spoke into the microphone in a slow, deep voice. He said, 'I would like to welcome you all to the National Museum. We are very proud to be holding this exhibition of art from Eastern Europe and Russia. I would like to extend our gratitude to everyone who has loaned works to the museum and helped to make this

11

such a wonderful show. But there is one person whom I would particularly like to thank. That person is King Jovan of Stanislavia.'

King Jovan was a small man with gold-rimmed glasses perched on his pointed nose. He was wearing a grey suit and black shoes.

His wife, Queen Rose, stood beside him. She was a tall, slim, elegant woman with long black hair. Around her neck, she wore a glittering necklace made from a hundred pearls.

'With exceptional generosity,' continued the Director, 'King Jovan has allowed us to show a work which has never previously been shown anywhere in the entire world. So, my friends, we are privileged to be here today. This is a historic event. For the first time in history, the public will have the chance to see this magnificent work of art, the Golden Dachshund. Today is a great day for our museum. I hope it is also a great day for the Golden Dachshund. Now, I should like to ask King Jovan to say a few words.'

Everyone clapped. The Director handed the microphone to King Jovan.

'Thank you very much,' said King Jovan. 'When my father fled from Stanislavia to the United States, he brought the Golden Dachshund in his luggage. Since his death, more than twenty years ago, I have been the keeper of the Golden Dachshund. Over those years, many different people have tried to buy it. I have been approached by private collectors, museums, even a sausage salesman. All of them have begged me to sell.

Only a month ago, I received an offer of ten million dollars.'

Around the room, people gasped in amazement.

'That's right,' said King Jovan. 'Ten million dollars.' He turned his head and smiled at the Golden Dachshund in its glass case. 'It's a lot of money. Particularly for a poor man like myself. But I said no to those ten million dollars. Just as I said no to all the other collectors and museums who begged me to sell this statue. I have always said no and I always will. The Golden Dachshund belongs to the people of Stanislavia. One day, it will be returned to its proper home, the Stanislavian National Museum in Vilnetto. Right now, I am very proud that the Golden Dachshund is on show in the American National Museum in New York.'

There was a round of applause. At the back of the room, a few people cheered.

'The Golden Dachshund will be on display for one month,' said King Jovan. 'Then it will be returned to its usual home. A bank vault. Inside the bank vault, it is completely secure, but it can be seen by no one. Such a magnificent work of art deserves to be seen. I hope many, many people come to this museum over the next month and see this beautiful sculpture for themselves. Thank you.'

There was another round of applause. King Jovan switched off the microphone. People started chatting amongst themselves, and drinking champagne, and eating the interesting snacks which the waiters were carrying on their trays.

*

'That looks good,' said Tim, pointing at one of the snacks. 'What is it?'

'Caviar,' said the waiter. 'On soda bread.'

'I'll try it,' said Tim. He took two.

When the waiter had gone, Tim ate one piece of caviar. He wrinkled his nose. It tasted fishy. He dropped the second piece on the floor. Grk jumped forward, grabbed the caviar between his teeth and swallowed it down in a single gulp.

Tim, Natascha and Max were standing at the back of the room. Grk was squatting at their feet, trying to avoid being stepped on.

They didn't know anyone at the party, but they were still having a good time. They eavesdropped on conversations. They stared at the pictures on the walls and the sculptures on the plinths. They gazed at the other guests, pointing out interesting sights to one another: a woman wearing a diamond tiara; a man with green hair; a pair of pointy shoes that you wouldn't be surprised to see on the feet of a witch.

'Let's go and see the Golden Dachshund,' said Max. Without waiting for a reply, he started pushing through the crowd, heading for the middle of the room.

Natascha, Tim and Grk followed him, easing through the forest of arms and legs and bodies. Someone spilt champagne on Tim's head. Someone else trod on Grk. But they finally reached the plinth in the middle of the room and stared through the glass at the Golden Dachshund.

14

The Golden Dachshund was the same size and shape as most other dachshunds. It had a long body and short legs. Its snout was slim and its ears were pointed. If you were being cruel, you might have said that it looked a little like a sausage on sticks. But there was one vital difference between the Golden Dachshund and just about any dog on the planet. Rather than blood and muscle and flesh and fur and teeth and claws, this particular dachshund was made from solid gold, which glittered in the museum's strong lights.

Tim looked down at the floor. Beside his feet, he could see Grk snuffling and chewing something. He said, 'Hey! What's that?'

Grk looked up with a guilty expression on his face. His jaws stopped moving.

'Don't pretend you're not eating,' said Tim. 'Open your mouth.'

Grk kept his mouth tight shut.

Tim squatted on the floor, grabbed Grk's jaws with both hands, and pulled them apart. 'I said, open! Come on, Grk. Open!'

Slowly, reluctantly, Grk opened his mouth.

Inside, Tim could see something pink.

Natascha squatted beside him. She said, 'What is it?'

'I don't know,' said Tim. 'Looks like a frankfurter.'

Natascha said, 'Where would he get a frankfurter?'

'Maybe one of the waiters gave it to him.'

'I suppose so.' Natascha shrugged her shoulders. 'Oh, well. It can't do him any harm. Let him eat it.'

Tim released Grk's jaws.

Grk chomped the frankfurter and swallowed it down before they could change their minds.

Have you ever squatted on the floor in the middle of a crowded room, watching a small dog eat a frankfurter?

If you have, you'll know that it's quite a dangerous thing to do. With so many people surrounding you, and most of them so much taller than you, no one can see you. You run the risk of being squashed. A waiter with a tray of glasses might trip over you. A heavy man with huge boots might step on your head. Or two people might shuffle past, not noticing you, and have a conversation that they didn't particularly want you to hear.

That was what happened to Tim and Natascha.

They were squatting on the floor in the middle of the party, watching Grk swallow a sausage, when two people pushed through the crowd and stood beside the statue of the Golden Dachshund.

'Sausage salesman,' said one of the people in a low, angry voice. He was an overweight man with a red face and an angry voice. 'Can you believe it? Sausage salesman. How dare he call me a sausage salesman!'

'Don't worry about him,' said the other person. He was a thin man with a quiet voice which would have been difficult to hear even if you had been standing right beside him. Tim and Natascha were squatting at his feet and, over the noise of the party and all the other conversations continuing around them, they could only hear about half of what he said. He muttered a couple of sentences which were completely impenetrable – Tim and Natascha heard the words 'night', 'million' and 'ready', but nothing else – and then he said, 'You'll get your revenge soon enough.'

'I certainly will.' The large man chuckled.

For a moment, the fat man and the thin man stared at the Golden Dachshund in silence.

Tim took the opportunity to observe them. For some reason, he was intrigued by them. He would have liked to see their faces.

The thin man was exceedingly thin. He was wearing a black suit and black leather boots. He had short black hair.

The fat man was exceedingly fat. His big puffy limbs were encased inside a tight white suit. He was wearing white leather shoes with white laces and white socks. He had curly blond hair.

After a few seconds of silence, the fat man turned to the thin man and said, 'You sure you can do it?'

'Of course I can do it,' said the thin man.

'When are you going to do it?'

'It's probably better if you don't know.'

'Yeah, whatever,' said the fat man. He reached into his pocket and pulled out two frankfurters wrapped in white paper. As he popped one of them into his mouth, the other dropped to the floor.

Grk had been watching carefully. Now he took his chance. He jumped forward with his mouth open.

The fat man turned round. Reaching out with his fat

fingers, he leaned down to retrieve his missing frankfurter, and came face to face with a small white dog.

Neither of them moved.

While the man and the dog stared at one another, Tim inspected the man's face. It was red. His cheeks were red, his eyes were red and his mouth was red. There were only two parts of his head which weren't red – his mop of blond hair and his blond bushy moustache.

Very suddenly, Grk lunged forward, grabbed the frankfurter between his jaws, turned round and ran. Two seconds later, he had disappeared through the crowd of legs.

The fat man blinked. He couldn't quite believe what had just happened. Then he saw something else which he couldn't quite believe either. He lifted his eyes and realised that two children were sitting on the floor, staring at him.

'I'm very sorry,' said Tim. 'I'll buy you another frankfurter.'

'He doesn't normally behave like that,' said Natascha. 'He's really a very good dog.'

'Whatever,' said the fat man, waving his right hand dismissively, as if he was brushing them away. He touched his companion on his elbow and said something that the children could not hear. The two of them, the fat man and the thin man, pushed through the crowd and walked away.

Tim and Natascha looked at one another. 'He wasn't very nice,' said Tim.

'He was horrible,' said Natascha. 'Let's find Grk.'

Near the exit, they found Max standing on his own, not talking to anyone. He looked bored. Grk was sitting at his feet.

The four of them lingered there for a few minutes, watching the crowds, waiting for Mrs Malt to finish her conversation with the Russian Cultural Attaché and Mr Malt to finish his conversation with a senior partner of the Bulgarian National Bank.

When those conversations had reached their conclusions, the Malts, the Raffifis and Grk left the museum. They walked down the street to a Japanese restaurant recommended by the guidebook. Tim had never eaten sashimi before and the thought of putting a raw fish in his mouth didn't really appeal to him. But to his surprise, it was quite nice.

Chapter 4

If you were a guard at the National Museum, you had a choice of three daily shifts. Tony Cserkesz had been working at the museum for two years and he still hadn't decided which of the shifts was worst. Or which was best.

If you did eight in the morning till four in the afternoon, you shared the museum with all the tourists and had to answer their dumb questions. But at least you got home in time to see your kids before they went to bed.

If you did four in the afternoon till midnight, you missed having dinner with your family. But at least you got a decent night's sleep.

If you did midnight till eight in the morning, you'd spend the following day asleep, while everyone else was awake. But at least you didn't have to see any tourists or answer their dumb questions.

Because he couldn't decide which shift was best, Tony Cserkesz liked to swap around and do some day shifts, some evening shifts and some night shifts. Today, the day after the grand opening of the new Slavic Art exhibition, he was doing the evening shift. He arrived at the museum at four o'clock in the afternoon, while a few visitors were still touring the galleries. He answered some dumb questions from tourists. He took a trip to the new exhibition and had a quick look at the solid gold statue that everyone was talking about. His Aunt Phyllis used to keep dachshunds. Strange little dogs, Tony thought. Personally, he preferred cats.

When the museum closed at six o'clock, Tony toured the galleries, making sure no dumb tourists had managed to get themselves locked inside. You'd be amazed how often that happened. Using his special key, he switched on the alarms. Then he retired to the control room and joined the other three guards on duty.

Around them, fifteen screens showed every angle of the National Museum, inside and out, relaying images from a hundred cameras. Every two seconds, the picture on each camera changed, showing another room, another window, another view.

You couldn't watch the screens all the time. You'd go crazy. To pass the time, Tony and the other guards played some poker and drank some coffee, glancing at the screens every few seconds.

At midnight, the next shift arrived. Tony put on his coat, covering his uniform, and walked down to the street with the other guards. They had cars, but Tony preferred to walk home. He liked the fresh air.

He walked to the end of the block, whistling to himself. Another shift finished. Another few dollars earned. He was saving up for a holiday. When he had a thousand spare dollars, he was going to take his wife and the kids to Florida for a week. Go see Disney World.

On the corner, a thin man in a black suit was standing in the shadows. He had a peaked cap on his head. Because of the angle of the shadows, Tony couldn't see his face.

The thin man had a cigarette in his left hand. As Tony approached, the thin man said, 'Excuse me, my friend, do you have a match?'

'Sorry,' said Tony. 'Don't smoke.'

'Why does no one in this city smoke?'

'I guess we're all too concerned about our health,' said Tony. 'Good night.'

Tony continued down the street, smiling to himself, remembering his own attempts to smoke. He had only smoked three cigarettes in his entire life. He'd wanted to know what all the fuss was about. But the smoke just made him feel sick. He tried three cigarettes, almost killed himself with all the coughing, and decided never to try another. One of the best decisions of my life, thought Tony.

At that moment, his world went black. He felt a terrible pain at the back of his head. And then he didn't feel anything at all.

Tony sighed and fell forwards, unconscious.

Before Tony hit the ground, the thin man caught him and dragged him into the shadows.

Three minutes later, the thin man emerged from the shadows, wearing Tony's coat, Tony's hat and Tony's uniform. The trousers were a little baggy and the jacket was too long, but they looked no worse than most uniforms. The thin man walked briskly towards the museum, whistling to himself.

The four guards on the midnight shift had already settled

into their usual routine. One of them brought a pack of cards. Another brought a thermos of coffee. The third brought ham and egg sandwiches. The fourth brought a cheesecake. They sat round the table and played poker.

There was a loud buzzing sound. It was the intercom. The four guards looked at the camera and saw Tony.

That's not quite true. They didn't actually see Tony. They saw Tony's hat and Tony's jacket and Tony's coat and Tony's museum pass with Tony's photo and Tony's identification number. And so they assumed, quite logically, that they were looking at Tony.

'Hi, guys,' said Tony – or a voice which sounded very much like Tony's voice. 'I've forgotten something. Will you let me back in?'

'Sure.' The nearest guard pressed the button, opening the main gate.

On the cameras, the four guards watched Tony stepping through the gate, making his way across the main entrance, entering the lobby, climbing the stairs and walking towards the control room.

But when he came into the control room, all four guards stared at him in amazement. For one thing, the man wearing Tony's uniform wasn't Tony. For another thing, his face was hidden behind a gas mask. And for a third thing, he was holding a grenade.

The four guards started shouting. One of them grabbed a telephone. Another lunged for his truncheon A third jumped forwards with both fists raised. The fourth reached for the panic button under the desk.

But none of them was fast enough.

The thin man threw the grenade on the ground. It exploded. Gas filled the control room. The four guards stumbled backwards, holding their mouths and noses, coughing and choking. A moment later, all four were lying on the floor, unconscious.

The thin man walked out of the control room and hurried through the museum.

He walked quickly through the galleries until he reached the exhibition of Slavic Art. The three rooms were packed with extraordinary objects of inestimable value. There were paintings which had never previously left Russia. There were Bulgarian necklaces and Serbian swords and Ukrainian brooches and Polish portraits which were worth millions of dollars. The thin man ignored all of them and headed for the large glass case which contained the Golden Dachshund.

He took the truncheon from his back pocket. He drew back his arm. He smashed the truncheon into the glass case.

As the glass exploded into a thousand pieces, a high-pitched alarm went off. Lights started flashing. Metal bars slid over the windows.

The thin man reached through the hole in the glass, grabbed the Golden Dachshund with both hands, and started running.

The alarm was connected to the headquarters of the New York Police Department, alerting them that the museum was being attacked. Immediately, a radio message was broadcast over the police radio, calling all units within a five mile radius, ordering them to go directly to the museum.

Four minutes later, the first police car arrived outside the museum. Two minutes after that, three police cars had blocked the front entrance. Three more blocked the back. Officers spread through the streets, surrounding the museum, stopping anyone from coming in or going out.

But they were too late. The Golden Dachshund had gone.

Chapter 5

The Malts, the Raffifis and Grk emerged from the subway at 86th and Broadway. At the exit, Mr Malt stared at his map, then stared at the streets, trying to orientate himself.

By the side of the road, there was a stall selling magazines and newspapers. 'Look,' said Max. 'It's on the front page.'

Max, Natascha and Tim clustered round the stall, reading the front pages of the newspapers. Each paper reported the theft in a completely different way.

The headline on the front page of the *New York Times* was:

$20M STATUE STOLEN FROM NATIONAL MUSEUM

The headline on the front page of the *New York Post* was:

DOG-GONE! GOLD POOCH VANISHES IN MIDNIGHT RAID!

The headline on the front page of the *National Enquirer* was:

ALIENS STOLE MY DACHSHUND!

They read the stories quickly, trying to discover any information about the theft that hadn't already been broadcast on the TV news.

The theft had taken place between one and two o'clock in the morning. The thieves had disabled the museum's alarm system and knocked out five guards. One was still in hospital. The thieves had taken the Golden Dachshund and nothing else.

'I don't understand,' said Tim. 'According to the *New York Times*, the Golden Dachshund is worth twenty million dollars. The *New York Post* says thirty million. But in the museum, King Jovan said it was worth ten million.'

Max said, 'Maybe no one really knows what it's worth.'

'All art is like that,' said Natascha. 'Because art has no intrinsic value.'

Max and Tim stared at her. Max blinked a few times and rubbed his head. Tim said, 'What are you talking about?'

'It's very simple,' said Natascha. 'The value of any work of art is determined only by what someone is prepared to pay for it. Therefore, that value is entirely arbitrary. Because a work of art has no specific function, it has no intrinsic value.'

Tim and Max looked at one another. Max said, 'Do you understand her?'

'No,' said Tim. 'Do you?'

'Not at all,' said Max. 'And she's my sister.'

Natascha started to explain for a third time, but more slowly and with even shorter words, when Mr Malt

27

clapped his hands together. 'Come on, this way,' he cried. 'Three blocks, then two blocks. Hurry or we'll be late. Come on!'

He sped down the street, waving his map like a flag. The others followed close behind him. As they walked, Natascha tried explaining to Tim and Max exactly what she had meant, but they begged her to stop. Their brains were hurting.

Tim said, 'Natascha, do you know what your problem is?'

'No,' said Natascha.

'You read too many books.'

Natascha shook her head. 'Do you know what your problem is, Tim?'

'No,' said Tim.

'You don't read enough.'

Following Mr Malt's directions, they walked three blocks, turned right and walked two more blocks, and reached the Bramley Building, home to some of the richest and most influential families in New York.

As the Malts and the Raffifis approached the entrance to the Bramley Building, Grk stopped and sniffed the pavement.

'Come on,' hissed Tim. 'You don't need a pee. Not here.'

But Grk wasn't going to be dissuaded. He pulled the lead with all his strength.

'Oh, all right,' said Tim. 'Have a pee, then. If you're quick.'

He hurried after Grk, who snuffled along the

pavement, following a trail of scent. Beside a fire hydrant, Grk saw what he was looking for. He sprang forward and grabbed it in his teeth.

Tim said, 'What's that? What is it?'

Grk chewed quickly, trying to swallow whatever he had found as quickly as possible.

'Show it to me,' said Tim. He knelt on the pavement and grabbed Grk's jaws with both hands. 'Open. Come on, Grk. Open!'

Slowly and reluctantly, Grk parted his jaws and opened his mouth.

On Grk's tongue, Tim could see something pink. He'd seen something very similar somewhere before, and not very long ago. What was it? And where had it been? Then he remembered. 'That's another frankfurter,' he said. 'Where did you get that?'

Grk didn't answer. He just tried to swallow the frankfurter. But he didn't have any success, because Tim was holding his jaws.

'Tim! What are you doing! Come on, Tim!'

It was his mother's voice. She was standing near the entrance to the Bramley Building, beckoning furiously.

Tim sprang to his feet and ran towards his mother, pulling Grk on the lead. Grk swallowed the frankfurter in one gulp, licked his lips and sprinted to keep up with Tim.

The door of the Bramley Building was opened by a doorman wearing a long black coat with bright silver buttons. 'Good afternoon,' said the doorman in a deep

29

voice. 'Welcome to the Bramley Building.' He ushered them into the lobby and closed the door. 'My name is Roderick. I'm the chief doorman. How can I help you today?'

'We're here to see King Jovan,' said Max.

The doorman blinked. 'King who?'

'King Jovan of Stanislavia. And his wife, Queen Rose. We have an appointment to see them at half past four.'

'Ain't no kings living here,' said the doorman. 'No queens neither. You must have the wrong address.'

Mrs Malt cleared her throat. 'I think you may know them under a different name. Do Mr and Mrs Castle live in this building?'

'The Castles? You're here to see the Castles?'

'That's right,' said Mrs Malt. 'They're expecting us.'

'Well, why didn't you say so? I'll let them know you're here.' The doorman retreated behind his desk and picked up a phone.

As the lift rattled upwards to the fifteenth floor, Mrs Malt licked her fingers and smoothed down Tim's hair. 'Now, remember,' whispered Mrs Malt. 'You address him as "Your Majesty". And her as "Your Royal Highness".'

'You've already told me that,' said Tim. 'About a hundred times.'

'Well, this is the hundred and first. Tuck your shirt in.'

'Yes, Mum,' said Tim, and tucked his shirt in.

'And don't bite your fingernails.'

30

'No, Mum,' said Tim with a sigh.

'And, please, Tim, keep that dog under control.'

'He's fine,' said Tim, glancing at Grk. 'Aren't you?'

Grk wagged his tail.

That morning, Grk had been bathed and brushed. His nails had been clipped and his teeth had been scrubbed. He was wearing a brand new leather collar. In all his life, he had never been so clean. But he didn't intend to stay clean for much longer. As soon as he could, Grk was going to find a muddy puddle and roll over and over and over. He wouldn't stop until his coat was completely covered in dirt and his new collar looked like an old collar.

The lift juddered to a halt. The door slid open. The Malts, the Raffifis and Grk stepped into the corridor.

Grk sniffed the air. Somewhere, not too far away, he could smell the distinctive aroma of dachshunds.

They walked along the corridor to apartment 153. Mr Malt rang the bell. A few moments later, a short woman opened the door. She was wearing a black dress and a little white apron. She smiled and said, 'Can I help you?'

'Hello,' said Max. 'We've come to see King Jovan.'

Mrs Malt stepped forward and said, 'We've come to see Mr and Mrs Castle.'

'Please, come in,' said the woman. She was the maid.

She took their coats and led them through the apartment to a large room with long windows overlooking the city. At one end of the room, a painting of a mountain hung above a large fireplace. There were bookshelves on either side of the fireplace, and long leather sofas, and a coffee table laden with little silver knick-knacks.

'Wait here, please,' said the maid. 'I'll fetch Mr and Mrs Castle.'

Tim stared out of the window at the skyline of New York City. Among the forest of skyscrapers, he recognised the unmistakable silhouette of the Empire State Building.

Mr and Mrs Malt peered at one of the paintings and talked in whispers, each of them trying to decipher the signature in the bottom left-hand corner.

Natascha read the titles of the books in the bookshelf.

Max paced up and down the carpet. He was nervous. Coming here had been his idea. He had phoned the King and Queen, and asked for an appointment, explaining that he had something to say about the theft of the Golden Dachshund. And now that he was actually here, waiting to meet them for the first time, he hoped that he wasn't going to make a fool of himself.

Chapter 6

The King and Queen of Stanislavia lived in apartment 153, the Bramley Building, New York. But the nameplate on their door didn't say 'King Jovan and Queen Rose' or 'The Royal Family of Stanislavia' or even 'Their Majesties'. The carved letters on the bronze nameplate simply said 'Mr and Mrs Castle'. That was what the doorman always called them. So did the boy who delivered the *New York Times* every morning, and the woman who brought a box of fresh vegetables on Fridays, and the man who came twice a year to tune the piano.

King Jovan and Queen Rose had both been born in the USA, and they rarely used their royal titles.

Stanislavia is a small, mountainous country in the part of Eastern Europe which is closest to Russia. For many centuries, the Royal Family ruled Stanislavia, taking all the country's wealth for themselves and letting their subjects languish in miserable poverty. It shouldn't have been a surprise to them when the Stanislavian population rose up in fury and overthrew the monarchy.

The day after the revolution, the King and Queen fled from Stanislavia in their Royal Mercedes. The boot was stuffed with all the gold, silver and jewellery that they had managed to grab from the Royal Treasury. At the bottom of the boot, wrapped in a cashmere scarf and hidden in a suitcase, there was the Golden Dachshund.

They drove across Europe, boarded a steamer in Hamburg and sailed across the Atlantic. After two weeks of stormy seas, the steamer docked in New York. The King and Queen had been planning to stay for a day or two before continuing to Los Angeles, but they liked the look of New York and decided to live there.

A few years later, they had a son, their only child. They wanted to give him a good Stanislavian name. So they called him Jovan.

When his father died, Jovan became King of Stanislavia, although he had never even set foot in the country. Two years later King Jovan married a Texan girl named Rose, and she became his Queen.

Today, King Jovan works as a computer salesman. Queen Rose breeds dachshunds. Neither of them speaks a single word of Stanislavian.

Chapter 7

King Jovan and Queen Rose walked into the room, followed by five dachshunds. They were accompanied by two men, one wearing a black suit and one wearing a grey suit.

The dachshunds had little tartan coats and diamond-studded collars. Three of the dachshunds were black and two were brown. All five took one look at Grk and started yapping at the top of their lungs.

Some dogs would have run away. Others would have cowered or cringed or hidden. Not Grk. He opened his mouth and barked back just as loudly, making as much noise on his own as all the five dachshunds put together.

'Your Majesty,' said Mrs Malt, making a little curtsey. 'Your Royal Highness. How delightful to meet you.'

But the six dogs were barking so loudly, no one heard her.

Natascha was the first person to react. She grabbed Grk with both hands and hurried out of the room, carrying him like a baby.

When Grk had gone, the dachshunds shut up. For a second, the silence was so surprising that no one spoke. Then King Jovan said, 'So, you must be Mr and Mrs Malt. Welcome to our home.'

'Thank you, your Majesty,' said Mrs Malt. 'Thank you so much.' She curtseyed again.

King Jovan gestured to the men in suits. 'Let me introduce Detective Worst and Mr Snag.'

'Hello,' said the man in the black suit. 'My name is Detective John Worst. I'm conducting the criminal inquiry into the theft of the Golden Dachshund. Thank you very much for taking the time to talk to us.'

'And I'm Theodore W. Snag,' said the man in the grey suit. 'I'm with the Cumberland Fire & Theft Insurance Company. We're responsible for insuring the Golden Dachshund. As you can imagine, we are very eager to secure its return. So we would also be very grateful for any help that you could give us.'

They all shook hands with one another, then sat down on the two long leather sofas. The maid brought tea and cheesecake on a silver tray. The five dachshunds lay on the floor, turning their heads from side to side and sniffing the air, searching for Grk.

But Grk was safely locked in the kitchen, where Natascha had left him with a bowl of water and strict instructions to keep quiet.

King Jovan looked at Max. 'So, you're Max Raffifi? The son of the famous Gabriel Raffifi?'

'I am,' said Max.

'It's a great honour to meet you,' said King Jovan. 'When we spoke on the phone, you said you have a suspicion who has stolen the Golden Dachshund.'

'That's right,' said Max. 'I do.'

The King, Detective Worst and Theodore W. Snag leaned forward, eager to hear what Max said.

'Tell us everything,' said Detective Worst, opening his notebook and taking the lid off his pen. 'Whatever you know. Even if it doesn't seem important. The slightest scrap of information may help us in our enquiries.'

'There's only one person who would steal the Golden Dachshund,' said Max. 'And that is Colonel Zinfandel. He would do absolutely anything to get his hands on the Golden Dachshund.'

Colonel Zinfandel was the cruel and vicious dictator who ruled Stanislavia. With the assistance of his Secret Service, he had inflicted innumerable horrors on the miserable population.

That was enough reason for anyone to hate him. But Max and Natascha had another reason too. Colonel Zinfandel had been responsible for the murder of their parents.

Detective Worst said, 'You know this guy? This Colonel?'

'I have met him,' said Max. 'So has my sister.'

'You'd recognise him?'

'Definitely.'

'This is very interesting,' said Detective Worst. 'And what's his motive?'

'Money,' said Theodore W. Snag. 'It has to be money.'

Max shook his head. 'Colonel Zinfandel doesn't need money. He has enough. And when he needs more, he can always steal from the people of Stanislavia. No, what he wants is power. He would do anything to make himself look like the rightful ruler of Stanislavia. And that includes stealing the Golden Dachshund.'

Detective Worst leaned forward. 'Max, this is very interesting. It's a good theory. But do you have any proof?'

Max shook his head. 'No.'

'Well, without any proof, there's not much we can do. You understand that, don't you?'

'Yes,' said Max.

'Thank you for your time.' Detective Worst closed his notebook. 'Let's meet again on Monday afternoon. If you have any other thoughts between now and then, please call me. This is my number.' He took a card from his pocket and handed it to Max.

'I'll certainly call you,' said Max, taking the card. 'But I can't meet you again on Monday. We're going back to London tomorrow.'

'I'd be grateful if you could stay in New York for a few days,' said Detective Worst. 'If Colonel Zinfandel really is involved in this theft, then I'd like to be able to question you further. You're one of the few people in this city who has actually met him.'

Max looked at Mr and Mrs Malt. 'Could we change the tickets?'

'I don't know,' said Mrs Malt. 'And even if we could, I don't think we should. You're meant to be back at school on Monday.'

'If you don't mind me saying so, these kids can go to school anytime,' said Detective Worst. 'But we've got to find this sculpture as soon as possible. Most likely, the thieves will try to smuggle it out of the country. And when that happens, we don't have much hope of finding it again.'

38

Max said, 'If Colonel Zinfandel didn't steal it, then who did?'

'We're working on some leads,' said Detective Worst.

'Like what?' said Max.

'This isn't the first dachshund to be stolen. A bunch of pictures of dachshunds have gone missing from museums. One by a guy named ... Let me see.' Detective Worst pulled out his notebook and flicked through the pages till he found the name that he wanted. 'Hans Holbein. And another by Leonardo da Vinci. You know that guy? He did the Mona Lisa, right? Well, he painted a dachshund too, and someone stole it. Maybe there's an art collector out there, stealing pictures of dachshunds, and they wanted this sculpture for their collection. Or maybe someone took it for the gold. The statue is worth ten million dollars, but the gold, just the gold, melted down, might be worth five hundred thousand. And there are a lot of people who wouldn't say no to five hundred thousand dollars.'

King Jovan looked horrified. 'Do you really think it's been melted down?'

'That's a definite possibility,' said Detective Worst, 'which is why we have to move quickly.' He turned to Mr and Mrs Malt. 'Please, ring Max's school in England, say he's staying here for a few days. And his sister too. The New York Police Department would be very grateful for your co-operation. Can you do that?'

Mr and Mrs Malt looked at one another. Mr Malt shrugged his shoulders. 'I don't see why not,' he said.

Chapter 8

They returned to the Millard Fillmore Inn. From their room, Mr Malt rang his work and arranged to take a few days off. Then he rang Max and Natascha's schools and explained that they would have to stay in New York for a few more days. Tim volunteered to stay too, but his parents vetoed that idea.

That night, they went to Chinatown and had a meal in a restaurant recommended by King Jovan. 'If it's good enough for the Royal Family,' said Mr Malt, 'then it's good enough for us.' They ate several dishes that Tim had never seen before – sliced lotus roots, dan dan noodles, soft-shell crabs, sweet and sour crispy carp – and all of them were delicious.

The following morning, Tim, Grk and Mrs Malt hailed a taxi outside the Millard Fillmore Inn and drove to JFK. Mr Malt, Max and Natascha stayed behind.

The drive from the hotel to the airport took about an hour. Tim stared out of the window and thought about the unfairness of life. Tomorrow morning, when Tim went back to school, Max and Natascha would still be in New York. It just wasn't fair.

At the airport, Mrs Malt paid the taxi driver and found a trolley for their luggage. They went through the door marked DEPARTURES.

When they had checked in, Mrs Malt asked Tim if he'd like some food or drink. Tim shook his head. He was feeling too grumpy for eating, drinking or speaking.

Mrs Malt went to look at perfumes in the Duty Free shop. Tim and Grk wandered through the departure lounge. Tim looked at shops selling gadgets, T-shirts, CDs, DVDs and other trinkets for busy travellers who had forgotten to buy presents for the folks back home. Grk sniffed the floor, searching for scraps of food that other people might have dropped.

Suddenly, Grk lifted his head and sniffed the air.

Tim looked at Grk. 'What is it?'

Grk hurried forwards. He didn't get very far, because the lead was attached to his neck. But he pulled as hard as he could.

'All right,' said Tim. 'We'll go that way. If you really want to.'

They walked through the departure lounge, past the bookshop and the café, until they found a stall selling hot dogs.

Grk looked up at Tim and wagged his tail hopefully.

Tim shook his head. 'Sorry, Grk. I know how much you love sausages, but I'm not buying you a frank-furter.'

Grk kept staring at Tim with his big, sad eyes.

'There's no point staring at me like that,' said Tim. 'I don't have any money.'

Grk kept staring plaintively at Tim. His eyes seemed to get even bigger and sadder.

Tim said, 'Anyway, haven't you had enough

41

frankfurters? If you eat too many sausages, you'll get fat. Don't look at me like that, it's true. You had two in the museum. And then you found the one...' Tim's voice dried up. 'Frankfurters,' he whispered. 'Oh, gosh.' He laughed. 'You're a genius! You are an absolute genius!' He knelt down and stroked the top of Grk's head. 'And I think you might be a brilliant detective too. Yes! It's the frankfurters! It must be something to do with the frankfurters.'

He thought through the events of the previous few days. He remembered the museum and the Bramley Building and the frankfurters that Grk had found in both places. He remembered the fat man with the red face who had been so rude. He remembered the fat man's thin companion. He nodded. 'That's the connection,' he whispered to Grk. 'The fat man who was eating frankfurters. He and the thin man must have been working for Colonel Zinfandel. All we have to do is discover who they are, and then we've found the Golden Dachshund. Grk – you are a genius. Come on, let's tell Mum.'

He hurried through the departure lounge. Grk took one last look at the frankfurter stall, sniffed the air for a final time, then turned his back on those delicious-smelling sausages and trotted alongside Tim.

Mrs Malt was sitting on a bench, studying the two bottles of perfume that she had bought. 'Hello, sweetheart,' she said. 'Did you find anything nice?'

'I know who stole the Golden Dachshund,' said Tim.

'Do you?'

'Yes.'

42

'Who?'

'Whoever was eating the frankfurters.'

'Which frankfurters?'

Tim described the three frankfurters that had been eaten by Grk. First, there was the one that he found on the floor of the National Museum. Second, there was the one that the fat man dropped. Third, there was the one outside the Bramley Building. They just had to find the fat man who had been eating frankfurters, and they would have cracked the case. He crossed his arms and smiled confidently at his mother, awaiting her congratulations.

Mrs Malt sighed. 'Oh, Tim. I know you don't want to go back to school. I know you'd rather stay in New York with Max and Natascha. But this is ridiculous.'

'It's not ridiculous,' said Tim. 'It's the truth. I know it is. I've solved the case!'

'Let's see how you feel when you get back to London,' said Mrs Malt. 'If you're still so convinced about these frankfurters, we can ring Detective Worst and tell him your brilliant theory.'

'But we have to do something now,' insisted Tim. 'Don't you remember what he said? They have to find the sculpture as soon as possible. Otherwise, it's going to be melted down. Or smuggled out of the country.'

'I'm sure it can wait a few hours,' said Mrs Malt with a calm smile. 'Now, do you have enough to read on the flight? Or do you want to buy another book?'

Tim stared at his mother. He couldn't believe how short-sighted she was being. How could she talk about

43

books at a time like this? While they were chatting, the fat man and the thin man might be heating a flame under the Golden Dachshund, melting it down into liquid gold. Or they might be in this very airport, smuggling the Golden Dachshund aboard a plane.

'Sit down,' said Mrs Malt, patting the seat beside her. 'Now, I need your advice. This perfume costs half what it would in London. Should I buy more bottles? Or will two be enough?'

Tim sighed. He sat down beside his mother and said, 'How much do you use?'

'A bottle usually lasts two months.'

'Then you don't need another bottle. Two is enough. You'll definitely go abroad again within the next four months.'

Mrs Malt nodded. 'Thank you, Tim. That's very good advice.' She glanced at her watch. 'The flight leaves in about an hour. Do you want a drink?'

'No, thanks,' said Tim.

'Sure?'

'I'm sure.'

'Let me know if you change your mind.' Mrs Malt stuffed the two perfume bottles into her bag and took out a copy of *Vogue*. She flicked through the pages, looking at pictures of skinny models in fancy clothes.

For a minute or two, Tim sat quietly beside his mother. He glanced over her shoulder at the glossy photographs. He stared at the other passengers in the airport. He thought about Max and Natascha, and King Jovan, and Detective Worst. He remembered the Golden

Dachshund. He wondered what type of people would smash a glass case in the National Museum and steal a statue that had been on display for everyone to see. He remembered the fat man who had been so rude to him and Natascha. And he decided that there was only one thing that he could possibly do.

An hour later, Tim was standing in a lift in the Bramley Building, heading towards the fifteenth floor, trying to imagine exactly how he was going to solve the mystery of the missing dachshund.

Chapter 9

Tim walked along the corridor to apartment 153 and rang the bell. A few moments later, the maid opened the door. 'Oh, hello,' she said. 'You're the boy from yesterday, aren't you?'

'That's right,' said Tim. 'I've come to see the King and Queen. I mean, I've come to see Mr and Mrs Castle.'

'They're walking the dogs in Central Park,' said the maid. 'You want to wait?'

Tim thought for a moment. He said, 'Have they been visited recently by anyone who ate frankfurters?'

The maid stared at him. 'Excuse me?'

'A fat man,' said Tim. 'Eating frankfurters. Has he been here?'

'Been here? Doing what?'

'Visiting the King and Queen,' said Tim. 'Visiting Mr and Mrs Castle.'

The maid shook her head. 'I'm sorry, I don't understand what you're saying.'

'It's very simple,' said Tim, who was beginning to get a little impatient. 'Have they been visited by a fat man with a red face and a blond moustache? He might have been with another man, a thin man with black hair. Do you remember? Please, it's extremely important.'

The maid shrugged her shoulders. 'You'll have to ask

Mr and Mrs Castle,' she said. 'This is private information. I can't tell you about their visitors.'

Tim begged her, explaining that the information was absolutely vital, but the maid could not be persuaded to change her mind. Even when Tim explained that he was searching for the stolen Golden Dachshund, the maid refused to help. She told him to come back later, when the Castles returned from their walk, and talk to them in person. 'Or you could find them in the park,' said the maid. 'They won't be far away.'

'Fine,' said Tim. 'I'll do that.' He almost added, 'Thanks a lot for being so unhelpful,' but stopped himself.

'I'll tell them you were here,' said the maid.

Tim turned to go. Then he remembered the taxi driver waiting downstairs. He said, 'I don't suppose you could lend me fifty dollars?'

The maid blinked and stared at him. 'Did you say fifty dollars?'

'Yes,' said Tim. 'You see, I need to pay the taxi driver.'

The maid rolled her eyes and shook her head as if she couldn't believe what the world was coming to. And she shut the door.

Tim sighed. He couldn't blame her. If a stranger asked him for fifty dollars, he would probably say no. He turned and walked slowly back to the lift, trying to imagine how he was going to pay the taxi driver.

If he was an adult, he would have had several ways to pay. He would have owned a credit card. Or he could have got money from a cash machine. Or he would have had something valuable – a phone, a wallet, an iPod – to give the driver as a deposit. But he had nothing. His pockets were empty and his mind was blank.

Tim pressed the button to summon the lift. He felt desolate. He would have to go to the police with the taxi driver. The police would contact his father, who would bring some money, pay the driver, and send Tim to the airport. No one would believe his theory about the frankfurters. No one would ever trust him again.

I'm an idiot, thought Tim. Why did I run away from Mum?

The lift arrived with a loud PING! The door slid open. Tim stepped inside.

As he reached forward to press the button marked 1, he heard a voice shouting: 'Hey, little boy! Wait! Little boy!'

It sounded like the maid. Maybe she wanted to get in the lift too.

Tim pressed the button to hold the door open and peered into the corridor. The maid was hurrying towards him. 'Wait,' she called out. 'Wait for me.'

For a second, Tim was tempted not to wait. After all, what had she done for him? But he kept his finger pressed on the button that held the doors open.

The maid arrived at the lift. She was panting from the effort of running down the corridor. She said, 'Here. Take it.' In her hand, she was holding a fifty dollar bill.

Tim's eyes widened. He said, 'Oh, thank you. Thank you so much.'

'No problem,' said the maid. 'You'll pay me back?'

'Of course I will.'

'Promise?'

'I promise,' said Tim.

'Okay.' The maid handed over the money. She smiled. 'Good luck.'

'Thank you,' said Tim. 'I don't know how to thank you enough.'

'You don't have to,' said the maid. 'Just pay me back. Bye-bye.' She smiled again and hurried back along the corridor to the apartment.

Chapter 10

Down in the street, Tim paid the taxi driver and apologised for not having enough for a tip. The driver seemed pleased just to be paid. 'Enjoy New York,' he said. 'Have a nice day!'

As the taxi eased into the traffic and drove away, Tim attached the lead to Grk's collar. They headed down the street, stopping on the first corner to ask directions from an old lady with a King Charles Spaniel. Grk and the spaniel sniffed one another suspiciously. The old lady said, 'Excuse me for asking, but are you from England?'

'Yes,' said Tim. 'From London.'

'What are you doing here?'

'I'm on holiday.'

'All on your own?'

'No,' said Tim. 'My parents are waiting for me in the park.'

'Oh, then you'd better hurry along.' The old lady pointed in the right direction and told Tim to walk for three blocks until he saw the entrance to the park.

Following the old lady's directions, Tim and Grk walked briskly down the block, crossed three busy roads and reached the park. It was bounded by a low wall. They went through a gate, headed along a path and found themselves in a pleasant tree-lined avenue. The sun was shining. People were lying on the grass, reading books. Couples strolled along the paths hand in hand. There was the sound of laughter and conversation.

Tim unfastened the lead from Grk's collar. He slung the lead around his own neck, looked down at Grk and said, 'Now, you have to do something useful. Find the dachshunds. Understand?'

Grk wagged his tail, but didn't move.

'Dachshunds,' said Tim. 'Dachshunds! Where are the dachshunds?'

Grk stared at Tim with a curious expression. He knew they were playing some kind of game, but he wasn't quite sure of the rules.

'Come on,' said Tim. 'Remember the royal dachshunds? Of course you do. The King and Queen have five little dachshunds. They barked at you. They wore silly little coats and posh collars. Remember? Where are they? Find the dachshunds! Find the dachshunds!'

Grk put his head on one side and stared at Tim.

'Oh, come on, Grk,' said Tim. 'Don't look at me like that. You know exactly what I'm talking about. Those funny little dogs. The ones that look like sausages. Where are they? Where are the dachshunds?'

Grk started sniffing the air, turning his head from side to side, as if he was searching for a particular scent.

'That's right,' said Tim. 'The dachshunds! Find the dachshunds!'

Grk barked twice, then started trotting along the path.

He had obviously caught a scent and was heading after it. Every few paces, he turned his head and glanced backwards to check if Tim was following him.

51

'Good boy,' said Tim, clapping his hands together delightedly. 'Find the dachshunds!' He started running along the path in pursuit of Grk.

Grk sped up. His legs moved faster. He bounded along the path, wagging his tail excitedly. His nose was in the air, sniffing every scent, searching for the one that he wanted.

Tim suddenly realised that Grk was about to disappear. If that happened, Tim would be left alone in the middle of Central Park.

Tim ran across the grass, turning his head from side to side, searching for Grk. Where was he?

There! A flash of white between the trees. A tail and two ears. Grk had stopped. He was waiting, looking backwards, checking that Tim was following him.

When Grk saw that Tim was just a few paces behind, he started running again.

As they plunged deeper into the park, the scent must have grown stronger and stronger, because Grk seemed to become increasingly confident of the route that he was taking. His tail wagged faster. His legs worked harder. He ran swiftly and surely in the direction of the smell.

Tim sprinted to keep up with him.

They ran through the park, dodging past joggers and cyclists and mothers with prams. They headed up hills and down valleys and through a tunnel under the road.

They ran round the perimeter of a lake. Ducks and rowing-boats paddled slowly on the water. On the other side of the lake, skyscrapers rose like watchtowers, inspecting every move that people made.

Beside a fountain, a busker was entertaining the crowds, playing the guitar and singing *Jailhouse Rock*. At his feet, there was a hat containing a few coins. Grk sprang over it. Tim ran round it. A few onlookers clapped and cheered. The busker bowed his head as if they were applauding him and continued singing.

On the other side of the fountain, people sat at tables outside a café. A sign announced bike rentals by the hour or the day. Two clowns with painted faces juggled with oranges and bananas. Behind them, a busy road cut through the middle of the park, filled with fast-flowing traffic.

Grk stopped before they reached the road. He turned to look at Tim. His tail wagging furiously, he waited for Tim's praise and approval.

Tim stopped beside Grk. Exhausted from running so far and so fast, he held his sides, gasped for breath and looked around the park, trying to see the five dachshunds.

But there was no sign of them. Tim couldn't see a single dachshund. Or King Jovan. Or Queen Rose.

He looked down at Grk. 'Where are they?'

Grk wagged his tail and sniffed the air.

'I don't understand,' said Tim. 'Where?'

Grk pawed the ground and pointed with his nose.

Nearby, a line of people were queueing beside a stall. A brightly-coloured umbrella hung over the stall. Smoke spiralled into the sky from the pans of frying onions and steaming sausages. A line of scarlet letters spelled out the stall's slogan: DOCTOR WIENER'S DOGS – THE

BEST HOT DOGS IN NEW YORK! – I'LL CURE
YOUR HUNGER!

Tim stared at the stall, trying to spot the Stanislavian
Royal Family, but he couldn't see any sign of King
Jovan or Queen Rose or their five dachshunds. He stared
at the umbrella and the smoke and the slogan shouting
Doctor Wiener's prescription for curing hunger. And
then he realised what was going on. 'Not frankfurters,'
sighed Tim. 'I didn't ask you to find frankfurters. I asked
you to find dachshunds.' He stared at Grk and shook his
head. 'Oh, you really are a useless dog!'

Grk's ears drooped. His big, sad eyes stared at Tim.
Then he dropped his nose down to the ground, slumped
forward and lay sadly on the grass.

Immediately, Tim felt guilty. 'I'm sorry,' said Tim. 'I
didn't mean to snap at you.' He sat down and stroked the
top of Grk's head. 'I'm not cross. I'm disappointed, that's
all. But you have to admit, I was very clear in my instructions. I didn't say "frankfurters". I said "dachshunds".'

Grk lifted his head and stared at Tim for a minute. He
opened his mouth, extended his small pink tongue and
licked Tim's hand.

Tim tickled Grk's ears.

Everything was forgiven.

They sat on the grass and looked around the park.
Overhead, the sun had slipped behind a thick layer of
clouds. A chilly breeze blew through the trees. Tim
stared at the people queueing to buy Doctor Wiener's
hot dogs.

Watching a plump man burying his teeth into a sausage, squirting yellow mustard over his cheeks, Tim realised he was starving. What could be nicer than a hot dog? A juicy frankfurter in a white bun, slathered with ketchup and fried onions.

But he had no money. He and Grk would just have to go hungry.

Once again, Tim felt helpless and hopeless. He didn't know what to do or where to go. There was no point asking Grk to find King Jovan's dachshunds. They had tried that once already, and it hadn't worked.

It was probably too late anyway. By now, Colonel Zinfandel's men would have smuggled the Golden Dachshund out of New York. There would be no trace left of them or their crime.

Perhaps I should just give up, thought Tim. Perhaps I should go to the hotel and find Dad. Mum might be with him by now. They're probably worried about me. I should go and tell them that I'm okay.

Tim didn't like giving up. But he couldn't imagine what else to do. He had failed. There was no point pretending that he hadn't.

Oh, well, he thought. It's better to be honest. I'll just go back to the hotel, find Mum and Dad, and admit I was wrong.

He pulled himself slowly to his feet. In a sad voice, he said, 'Come on, Grk. Let's go.'

He wandered towards the lake. The busker was playing a tune that Tim recognised, although he didn't know its name.

Grk stopped to sniff a patch of dirt on the pavement. He licked it. Then he bounded after Tim.

They had hardly walked fifty paces when a loud voice shattered the peace of the park. 'You! Hey, you! Stop right there!'

It didn't occur to Tim that anyone could be shouting at him, so he kept walking, his head down, lost in his own melancholy thoughts.

The voice shouted again, even louder. 'You! With the dog! Stop right there!'

Perhaps he does mean me, thought Tim. He stopped and turned round.

A large man in a black uniform was pointing at Grk. 'Is that your dog?'

Tim nodded.

'Put him on the leash,' said the policeman.

'Why?'

The policeman grimaced and spoke very slowly as if he was addressing an idiot. 'I – said – put – him – on – the – leash.'

Tim didn't like being treated like an idiot. But the policeman was not only taller than him and wider than him and undoubtedly a lot stronger than him, but he had a variety of terrifying objects attached to his belt, including handcuffs and a pistol. It was probably best, Tim decided, to do whatever the policeman asked. Tim whistled and called Grk, who was sniffing the base of a tree. 'Come here! Quick!' Grk had a quick pee, then trotted across the grass to Tim. 'Sit,' said Tim.

Grk stared at Tim without moving a muscle.

'All right, don't sit,' said Tim. He leaned down and fastened the lead to Grk's collar.

When the policeman was sure that the lead had been securely fastened, he nodded and led Tim to a signpost standing upright by the side of the path. He said, 'Can you read?'

'Of course I can read,' said Tim. 'I'm twelve years old.'

'Then read this.' The policeman pointed at the sign. Five lines of yellow text were printed in big letters on a green background.

NO riding bicycles, rollerskates, scooters, skateboards
NO ballplaying or frisbees
NO alcoholic beverages
NO littering
NO dogs off leash

Tim read the words twice, then turned to the policeman, and said, 'I thought this was meant to be the land of the free.'

'This is the land of the free,' said the policeman.

'Then why can't my dog walk without a lead?'

'Because even in the land of the free,' said the policeman, 'we have rules.'

'Then it's not exactly free, is it?'

The policeman shook his head. 'Come on, kid. Get moving. I have a job to do here.' He pointed at Grk. 'And keep that dog leashed, right?'

'I will,' said Tim. 'Thanks very much.' He smiled at the policeman, then turned and walked slowly away, tugging Grk after him.

After a few paces, Tim stopped, realising that he didn't know which way to go. Where was the Millard Fillmore Inn? He remembered its address: the corner of 49th Street and Eighth Avenue. But where was that?

Tim knew what you should do when you're lost. Ask a policeman.

He turned round and started walking back to the sign that he had just been forced to read.

The policeman had gone. Tim looked round. Ah! There he was! Talking to the man who ran the hot dog stall. They were arguing about something.

Tim stopped. He didn't want to interfere in their argument. He was quite frightened of the policeman, who looked even more scary now that he was angry. His face was red and he was waving both arms around.

The hot dog seller seemed to have reached the same conclusion as Tim and decided to do whatever the policeman wanted. He pulled a phone from his pocket. He made a quick call.

The policeman walked away. After a few paces, he stopped, turned around and crossed his arms over his chest. He was obviously going to wait and see what happened.

Tim tugged Grk's lead. 'Come on,' he said. Together, they walked slowly back to the policeman and stopped beside him. 'Excuse me?'

The policeman looked down at Tim and Grk. He

nodded and smiled. 'That's good,' he said. 'You put your dog on the leash.'

'I didn't know I had to,' said Tim. 'In England, dogs can run around in parks.'

'Really? I didn't know that. I've never been to Europe.'

'This is my first time in New York,' said Tim.

'You like it?'

'I like it very much.'

'Good.' The policeman nodded. Then he glanced at the hot dog stall. 'What's taking these guys so long?'

Tim said, 'What are they doing?'

'He doesn't have a licence,' said the policeman, pointing at the hot dog seller. 'He can't stop there without a licence. He has to move on. Just about once a month, the city takes Doctor Wiener to court for selling hot dogs without the requisite licence, but we never seem to get a conviction.'

'Oh,' said Tim, nodding, although he wasn't quite sure what the policeman was talking about.

The policeman shook his head. 'The amount of money he makes...It's criminal.'

'Who?'

'Doctor Wiener. They say he owns a penthouse on the Upper West Side. Filled with all kinds of art. You know, paintings by Picasso, the real deal. Someone told me – I don't know if this is true – he's obsessed with those little dogs that look like sausages. What are they called?'

'Dachshunds,' said Tim.

'That's right. Dachshunds. He has a whole penthouse

59

filled with pictures of dachshunds. What it must have cost him. You wouldn't have thought a man could make so much profit from illegal sausages, would you?'

'No,' said Tim. He stared at the hot dog stall. His stomach felt very empty. He remembered that he hadn't eaten for a long time. 'Are they good? The hot dogs?'

'Yeah, not bad.' The policeman shrugged his shoulders. 'I've had better.'

Tim nodded sadly. He was so hungry, he would happily have eaten any kind of hot dog. Even just a bun with some ketchup – that would be enough for him.

But his pockets were empty. And the hot dog seller didn't look like the type of man who would hand over free samples of buns and ketchup.

After a few minutes, a white van drove along the road and stopped beside the hot dog stall. The driver jumped out of the van and ran round to the stall. Together, the seller and the driver wheeled the stall to the van.

The policeman stayed there, his arms folded, watching the two men fix the hot dog stall to the back of the van. He wasn't going to leave until they had driven away.

As Tim watched the hot dog men attach the stall to the van, he thought through the events of the past few days. He remembered the three frankfurters that Grk had already eaten, the one outside the Bramley Building and the two in the National Museum. Then he remembered King Jovan's speech on the opening night of the exhibition. What had the King said? 'I have been approached by private collectors, museums, even a sausage salesman. All of them have begged me to sell.'

A sausage salesman, thought Tim.

A sausage salesman with an art collection. Filled with pictures of dachshunds.

And what about statues of dachshunds? Does he have any of them?

Tim felt a shiver run down the length of his spine. He remembered the fat man in the National Museum, and the words that he had said to his thin friend. 'Sausage salesman,' the fat man had said. 'How does he dare call me a sausage salesman?'

Tim looked at the policeman. 'What else do you know about Doctor Wiener?'

'I don't know nothing about him at all,' said the policeman. 'Except he sells a lot of hot dogs.'

'If he wanted something, would he steal it? Is he that type of man?'

'Sure, I guess so,' said the policeman. 'He doesn't have much respect for the law. Look at his business operation.' He pointed at the white van, the hot dog stall and the two men labouring to attach them together. 'There are a lot of decent, law-abiding guys trying to sell good hot dogs in this city. But they can't compete with a crook and a cheat like Doctor Wiener. Do you think he pays his taxes? Do you think his guys have health insurance? Is he running a legitimate operation? Personally, I doubt it.'

'Is he fat?'

The policeman stared at Tim. 'Excuse me?'

'Doctor Wiener,' said Tim. 'Is he a big man with fat hands and blond hair and a red face?'

'I don't exactly know,' said the policeman. 'But I've seen a photo of him once, and he looked a little like that, yes. Big guy. Fair hair. I guess you could say he was somewhat heavy, yes.'

Tim nodded. 'This is going to sound really weird,' he said. 'But I think Doctor Wiener might be involved in the theft of the Golden Dachshund.'

The policeman raised his eyebrows. 'That statue? The one taken from the National Museum?'

'Exactly,' said Tim. 'Listen, you have to help me. We've got to find Doctor Wiener. Let's follow those men.' He pointed at the hot dog salesmen. 'If we find Doctor Wiener, I think we might find the Golden Dachshund.'

The policeman grinned. 'Have you been reading too many comics?'

'No.' Tim sighed. 'It's not a joke.'

'I'm sorry, kid. I don't mean to ridicule you. But life isn't like that. I can't leave the park. If anyone finds that statue, it'll be a detective from the crime squad, not a kid with a dog and a cop who's been patrolling Central Park for the past six months.'

'We could try,' said Tim.

'We could,' said the policeman. 'But we're not going to. You should find your folks. Now, will you be okay on the streets? Shall I put you in a cab?'

'I'm fine, thanks,' said Tim, who had absolutely no intention of finding his parents. There was only one

62

person who he was planning to track down – and that person was the mysterious Doctor Wiener.

Tim realised what he had to do. Forget about Mum and Dad. Forget about hunger. Forget about thirst. Forget about everything – except following that hot dog van.

But how?

Could he get a taxi? No. Taxi drivers had caused him enough problems for one day.

Could he sneak inside the white van and get a free lift? No. Not with the policeman standing there.

Then what could he do? How could he possibly follow a white van through the streets of New York?

And then he remembered what he had seen only a few minutes ago, while he and Grk were running through the park.

Tim looked up at the policeman. 'I have to go now.' He hissed at Grk, 'Come on! Quick!' He pulled Grk's lead and hurried towards the fountain.

He had only taken four or five paces when the policeman shouted after him. 'Hey! Kid! Wait!'

Tim stopped. He turned round. What now? What had he done now?

'My name's Andy,' said the policeman, taking a card from his pocket. 'Andy Kielbasinski. That's my cell number. You get in trouble, you need a hand, you need anything, call me. Okay?'

'Thanks,' said Tim, taking the card. 'I'm Timothy Malt. But everyone calls me Tim.'

'Nice to meet you, Tim.'

'Nice to meet you too, Andy.'

They shook hands.

Then, without another word, Tim turned round, tugged Grk's lead, and started running as fast as he could. Grk galloped alongside him.

Andy Kielbasinski stared after them, blinking and surprised. ''Bye,' he said. 'Have a nice day.'

Neither Tim nor Grk heard him. They were already too far away. They leaped down the stairs that led to the fountain, sprang over the busker's hat and charged towards the café.

Chapter 11

Behind the café, forty or fifty bicycles were stacked together under a sign painted in big yellow letters.

DINO'S RENT-A-BIKE
SEE CENTRAL PARK FROM A SADDLE!

Dino was a small man with a kind face. He was wearing red sneakers, yellow dungarees and a blue cap. He had patches of black oil on his hands, his face and his dungarees.

He pulled a bike from the stack and wheeled it towards Tim. 'That should suit you,' he said. 'Nice little bike. Had new tyres last week. Runs like a dream. Try it out.'

Tim sat down on the bike. It was a perfect fit. His feet just touched the floor and his bum felt snug on the saddle.

Dino popped a helmet onto Tim's head and fastened the straps under Tim's chin. 'Perfect,' said Dino, taking a step backwards. 'You're ready to go. Where are your parents?'

'In the café.'

'You'd better fetch them. We're going to need a credit card as a deposit.'

'I don't have a credit card.'

Dino laughed. 'Yeah, I guessed that. Which is why I

suggested you fetch your parents. They have credit cards, right?'

Tim shook his head. 'No, they don't.'

'No credit cards? Are you sure?'

'I'm sure,' said Tim.

'Then I'm sorry,' said Dino. 'But you can't rent a bike. Unless you have two hundred dollars in cash. We need a deposit, you see. In case you decide not to bring back the bike.'

Tim bit his lower lip. He didn't have a credit card or two hundred dollars. And this time, he wasn't going to leave Grk behind as security. He thrust his hands into his pockets and found a piece of chewing gum, two doggie treats, some string, lots of fluff and his passport. 'Will you take this?' He offered the passport to Dino. 'Instead of a credit card.'

Dino shook his head. 'Sorry, kid. But that could belong to anyone.'

'No, it couldn't,' said Tim. 'It has my picture in the back. Look.' He opened the passport, showing the photograph of himself, and handed it to Dino. The photo had been taken two years ago, but still looked pretty much like him.

Dino took the passport and flicked through its pages, staring at the multi-coloured stamps which showed the different countries that Tim had visited. Dino closed the passport and stared at Tim for a few seconds, as if he was trying to reach a decision. Finally, he nodded. 'You have an honest face,' he said. 'I'll trust you.'

'Thank you,' said Tim. 'Thank you so much. I'll bring your bike back, I promise.'

'You'd better,' said Dino. He fetched the key for the bike's lock and a map. The location of Dino's Rent-A-Bike was marked with a big red star.

'Keep to the cycle paths', said Dino. 'Obey all traffic laws. And bring the bike back by six. Or I'll keep your passport.'

Dino put his hand on Tim's back and gave him a quick push, sending him and the bike whizzing along the path that led back to the heart of Central Park. Grk sprinted in pursuit.

As a policeman in New York City, you get to see just about everything. But this was something that Andy Kielbasinski had never seen before.

He was standing by the side of the road, watching the hot dog stall ease away from the pavement. He knew they would be back. Even if they didn't return to this exact spot, they would just stop somewhere else in the city and sell their unlicensed, illegal and probably poisonous hot dogs. But that wasn't his problem. He had forced them to leave Central Park, and he couldn't do any more than that.

The hot dog stall swung from side to side as the white van joined the traffic.

Just as Andy Kielbasinski was turning to walk away, something whooshed past him at great speed.

What was that?

A boy on a bike. Accompanied by a dog.

The bike and the boy and the dog whizzed past Andy Kielbasinski's legs. If they had been one inch closer, the rubber tyres would have run over the polished toes of his black boots.

The bike shot off the path, bumped down the edge of the pavement, skidded slightly on the tarmac, and sped after the hot dog van. A moment later, the van, the boy, the bike and the dog turned the corner, and all four vanished from sight.

Andy Kielbasinski blinked. Had he really seen that? Or was he dreaming?

You know, he thought to himself, this is exactly what I like about my job. Every day is different. Every day, I see something that I have never seen before.

He turned round and walked back into the park, resuming his patrol. Near the fountain, he saw a young woman dropping candy wrappers as she strolled across the grass. Immediately, Andy Kielbasinski forgot the boy and the bike and the dog, and concentrated on doing his job. 'Hey, you!' he shouted. 'Lady, pick up your litter!'

Cycling through the park was easy. Tim pedalled fast. The paths were wide. When people saw him coming, they got out of the way.

The bike came with a lock and a helmet, but no basket, so Grk had to run alongside, jogging briskly to keep up. But he was a fit young dog, so he didn't have any problems.

They circumnavigated the fountain and sped past the busker, slaloming round his coin-filled hat. They whizzed past Andy Kielbasinski, bumped off the edge of the pavement and joined the road.

That was when things started getting difficult.

There were five or six cars between Tim and the white van. He didn't want to go any closer than that, or the driver might notice that he was being followed. But he couldn't drop any further behind, or he would lose sight of the van completely. So he had to concentrate very carefully on pedalling at exactly the right speed, not too fast and not too slow, keeping pace with the van. At the same time, he had to avoid hitting a pedestrian or jumping a red light or smacking into the back of a taxi or falling off. And, while doing all that, he had to ensure that Grk didn't get run over.

Quite quickly, Tim had the sense that his brain wasn't big enough to process all the information flooding towards him. Cars and people, skyscrapers and shops, the sound of voices and engines and music – all of them jumbled together, smothering his senses. It felt as if there were a thousand different sounds, a thousand sights, a thousand smells, all rushing towards him, entering his eyes and ears and nose, filling him with sensations, pulling him in a billion different directions.

Tim tried to ignore all these sensations and concentrate just on the white van.

If the traffic had moved fast, he would have been left behind immediately. Fortunately, the whole of New York City seemed to be stuck in a huge traffic jam. The taxis, cars and trucks eased slowly forward, stopping at red lights, waiting for pedestrians, never travelling faster than five or ten miles an hour.

They turned a couple of corners, then headed in a straight line for a long time, working their way down Manhattan. The streets were numbered. After 57th Street, they crossed 56th Street, then 55th Street, and all the way down through the rest of the 50s, past 54th Street and 53rd Street and 52nd Street and 51st Street and 50th Street, then through the 40s and the 30s and the 20s, until Tim began to wonder what would happen when they crossed 3rd Street and 2nd Street and 1st Street. Would there be a Zero Street? And what would happen after that? Would they reach the end of the island and fall in the water?

Chapter 12

Tim's legs ached. He had been cycling for a long time. Beside him, Grk was puffing desperately, falling further and further behind. At each junction, Tim prayed that the lights would stay red for a little longer, giving him and Grk more time to catch their breath.

In the end, they didn't get as far as Zero Street. On West 8th Street, the white van turned a corner, then another, drove round a park and stopped beside a crowd of young men and women who looked like students.

Tim stopped about fifty feet away, close enough that he could see what was happening, but far enough away that he wouldn't be noticed. He jumped off the bike and sat on the curb, resting his exhausted legs. He undid the strap on his helmet and took it off. Lines of sweat dribbled down his forehead.

Tim was exhausted and thirsty. He would have been very happy to drink a bottle of cold water, then fall asleep. But he had no money to buy water and he couldn't go to sleep, not yet, not while Doctor Wiener's men were still working.

Grk didn't care about Doctor Wiener's men or anyone else. He flopped down on the pavement and closed his eyes. A moment later, he started snoring.

The white van's doors opened. The two men jumped

71

out, hurried round to the back of the van, and detached the hot dog stall. One of the men lifted the umbrella which displayed Doctor Wiener's slogan: DOCTOR WIENER'S DOGS – THE BEST HOT DOGS IN NEW YORK! – I'LL CURE YOUR HUNGER! The man started fiddling with switches on the hot dog stall. The other man opened the back of the van and removed several large plastic boxes. He lifted the lids, revealing stacks of sausages, buns and chopped onions.

Five minutes later, onions were frying and hot dogs were steaming. The students started queueing up to buy them.

Tim felt extremely envious. He would have given just about anything to be eating a hot dog, smothered in ketchup, rather than skulking in a doorway, watching other people have all the fun.

The driver clambered into the van and started the engine. Black smoke gushed out of the exhaust.

'Let's go,' said Tim, who was already slotting his helmet onto his head. He fastened the clasp, jumped onto his bike and grabbed Grk's lead.

The van eased away from the curb and roared into the traffic. Fifty feet behind, Tim put his feet on the pedals and urged his aching legs to start moving again. For the first few rotations, he really thought that his energy had run out. His muscles had no strength. His knees cracked. Sharp pains shivered along his thighs and calves.

I could give up now, thought Tim. I could turn round, head north and find the Millard Fillmore Inn. Dad would be there. He would be so pleased to see me, he wouldn't be cross that I'd run away. I could have a Coke and a chicken sandwich, then go to bed and watch telly till I fell asleep.

No, thought Tim. No giving up. No turning round. Not now.

The white van was ahead of him, turning the corner. Tim pushed down on the pedals, ignoring the protests of his exhausted legs and forcing himself to move faster.

Grk ran alongside him, panting for breath.

Both of them were so hungry, so thirsty and so tired, it was a miracle that they kept going.

They turned the corner and whizzed down the middle of the road, Tim pedalling and Grk galloping, overtaking lines of traffic, always keeping the white van in sight.

They followed the van through crowded shopping streets, around another park and onto Brooklyn Bridge.

At the very last moment, just before Tim cycled onto the bridge, he noticed a street sign ordering cyclists and pedestrians to take a raised walkway above the road. He did as he was told, pedalling hard to get up the initial slope. His legs protested, begging him to stop for a rest, but he ignored the sharp pains shooting along his calves and thighs and concentrated on the path ahead.

The wooden walkway went across the bridge on a higher level than the road. It was divided into two halves by a yellow line painted down the middle of the walkway. One side was for pedestrians and the other for cyclists.

On the road below, Tim could see the white van. It

was going faster than him, but there was a lot of traffic crossing the bridge, so he didn't fall too far behind.

A strong breeze blew off the river. Tim thought he could smell the sea, although perhaps he was actually smelling the salty sweat dripping off his own face.

He passed a huge brick arch, standing astride the bridge, and then another. A mesh of criss-crossing metal cables led to and from the arches. By the second of the arches, thirty or forty tourists dallied by the railings, taking photos of the skyline and one another.

Tim couldn't resist pausing just for a second to see what they were photographing. He whistled to Grk, warning him to stop, then jammed on the brakes and slid to a halt. He turned round and stared at the most magnificent view that he had ever seen.

On his left, jutting out of the hazy horizon, he could see the distant tiny figure of a woman holding a torch above her head.

On his right, standing tallest in a forest of skyscrapers, he could see the distinctive silhouette of the Empire State Building.

And ahead of him, he saw a hundred other towers, all different shapes and sizes, like a hundred massive fingers wriggling out of the earth and stretching towards the sky.

There was so much to see, so many wonderful sights to ogle, he would have been happy to stand there all day. Parallel with the bridge that he was standing on, for instance, there was another bridge, just like this one, with two solid arches and long powerful cables stretched

74

between them. Down below, ferries and speedboats scudded across the water. Up above, a couple of helicopters buzzed through the sky. On the arch itself, built into the brickway, there was a plaque, listing the names of the people who had built the bridge. Tim wanted to stop and read it.

But he couldn't waste another second. Not now.

He turned and peered over the edge, staring at the road below. Among the traffic, accelerating away from him, he could see the back of the white van. 'Quick, Grk,' said Tim. 'We've got to move. We're losing him.'

Grk looked up at him with despairing eyes.

But I'm happy here, Grk's expression seemed to say. Can't we lie down? Just for an hour or two? Even a couple of minutes?

'Sorry,' said Tim. 'We can rest later. Come on!' He pushed his feet down on the pedals and started cycling towards the other side of the bridge.

The lead went taut, then jerked Grk's collar. Reluctantly, Grk hobbled to his feet and started jogging behind the bike's back wheel.

On the other side of the bridge, the wooden walkway sloped downwards and rejoined the road leading into the heart of Brooklyn. Apartment blocks and factories hunched over the six-lane highway, staring down from a thousand blank windows.

Tim and Grk followed the van along the highway.

After ten minutes, the traffic cleared. The van roared ahead. There was no way that Tim could keep up, but he was determined to try. He pedalled as fast as he could, ignoring the pains shooting along his legs and through his lungs. Behind the back wheel, Grk galloped along the tarmac, exhausted and dirty and gasping for breath, but never complaining, never stopping, never giving up. Tim tried to empty his mind of all thoughts and concentrate on the steady rhythm of his feet, pushing down on the pedals, never stopping, never giving up.

Until the front tyre of Tim's bike rode over a nail which had been dropped by the side of the road.

The nail pierced the rubber tyre. With a loud BANG, the inner tube popped. Tim lost control of the bike. He swerved to the left, then the right, and flung his legs out to the sides, trying to avoid skidding into the middle of the traffic.

The front wheel turned back on itself, then crunched into the side of the road. Tim shot forwards. He spun through the air, toppling over the handlebars, and slapped down on the tarmac.

Grk rolled over and over and over, then banged against the curb and lay still.

On the six-lane highway, the traffic sped past.

Chapter 13

'Are you okay?' The voice was soft and kind. 'Can you hear me? Come on, little boy, talk to me. What's your name?'

'Urrrrr,' mumbled Tim.

'What did you say? Ernie? Is that your name? Ernie?'

Tim opened his eyes. He was propped against the railings that ran alongside the highway. His bike was lying beside him. He mumbled, 'Where's Grk?'

'Where's what, Ernie?'

Tim lifted his head and stared at the source of the voice.

A plump woman with blonde hair and big blue eyes was leaning over him. She smiled. 'Talk to me, Ernie. Can you move your arms and legs? Is anything broken?'

Tim said, 'Where's Grk?'

'Where's what?'

'My dog.'

'The dog?' The woman pointed. 'He's here.'

Grk was curled on the pavement beside Tim, licking his back paws.

'Hey, little dog,' whispered Tim. 'Are you okay?'

Grk's tail slapped against the pavement, but he didn't stop licking his back paws, cleaning all the dirt out of them.

The woman sat down on the pavement beside Tim and introduced herself. Her name was Sandra. She finished work an hour ago. She had been driving along the highway, heading home, when she saw that there had been an accident. She pointed at her station wagon, parked by the side of the road with its hazard lights flashing. 'I'll have to move it now,' she said. 'I'm blocking the lane. Let me give you a lift. Where do you live?'

'London,' said Tim.

'London, England?'

'Yes.'

'I'm not taking you there.' Sandra grinned. 'But I'll give you a lift to the subway.'

Tim looked around. Of course, there was no sign of the white van. He'd lost it. Perhaps if he kept going down the same road, he might find it, parked beside another hot dog van, delivering more sausages and mustard. That seemed pretty unlikely, but he couldn't think of anything else to do. He said, 'Thanks for your help. But I feel fine now. I'll just get on my bike.'

'I don't think your bike is going anywhere.' Sandra pointed at the jumbled mess that had once been a bicycle. The front wheel had snapped. Spokes pointed in all directions. The inner tube lay on the tarmac like a dead snake.

Tim wondered what he was going to tell Dino, the bike-rental man, and whether he would ever see his passport again. Dino would be perfectly entitled to keep it. What would Tim do without a passport? Would he be stuck in the USA for ever?

He remembered the other thing that Dino had given him: the helmet. He'd forgotten he was even wearing it.

He unclasped the strap and removed the helmet from his head. The plastic had been cracked in several places by the impact.

'That's a good advertisement for helmets,' said Sandra. 'If you hadn't been wearing a helmet, your skull would be cracked just like that.'

'I know,' said Tim, touching the wriggly cracks that ran along the helmet and imagining the same cracks running across his skull.

Sandra said, 'Arms? Legs? Everything else okay?'

Tim stretched his arms and legs, checking nothing was broken. 'I feel fine.'

'You sure? Because I could easily take you to the hospital. Get you checked out.'

'I'm fine,' said Tim.

Sandra put her fingers under Tim's chin and lifted his head. 'Are you really, truly, honestly sure? Because I don't like leaving you here.'

'I'm sure,' said Tim. 'Honestly.'

'Okay.' Sandra smiled. 'What were you doing in this part of Brooklyn, anyway? You're quite a way from London, England.'

'It's a long story,' said Tim. 'I was chasing a hot dog van.'

'One of Doctor Wiener's?'

Tim stared at Sandra in astonishment. 'How did you know?'

'Because his factory is right there.' She pointed through the railings behind them. 'It's one of the few landmarks we have.'

79

Tim turned to look. On the other side of the railings, through a jumble of warehouses and pylons, he could see a large building with an enormous advertising slogan painted in white letters on the brickwork: DOCTOR WIENER'S HOT DOGS – THE BEST ON THE PLANET.

Tim struggled to his feet. His legs ached, his arms were covered in bruises and a steady pain throbbed through his skull, but he was determined to reach the factory as quickly as possible. 'How do I get there?'

'I'll give you a lift,' said Sandra. 'It's not far off my route.'

'Brilliant, thank you. Can we go now?'

Sandra laughed. 'What's the hurry?'

'It's complicated,' said Tim. 'But very important.'

'That sounds fascinating. Tell me more.'

'I can't,' said Tim. 'I would if I could, but I can't.'

Sandra smiled. 'What if I said, I'll only give you a lift to the factory if you tell me why you want to go there?'

'Then I'll walk.'

Sandra smiled. 'You're a pretty cool kid, aren't you?' Without waiting for an answer, she grabbed Tim's broken bicycle and loaded it into the back of her station wagon.

They climbed into the front seats. Grk sat on Tim's lap. Tim fastened the seat belt so it covered them both.

Sandra drove fast. She took the next exit off the expressway. Five minutes later, they stopped outside Doctor Wiener's factory. It was surrounded by a high wall, topped with barbed wire. The only entrance was a solid metal gate.

At Tim's request, Sandra drove round the corner and parked the station wagon out of sight of the factory, where they couldn't be seen by the guards or the CCTV cameras. He didn't want to be spotted by anyone. Sandra opened the back of her station wagon, unloaded the smashed bicycle, shook hands with Tim and said, 'Good luck, Mister Mysterious. With whatever you're doing.'

'Thank you very much,' said Tim.

Sandra clambered back into the station wagon, waved her hand out of the window and drove away.

Chapter 14

The street was empty. A pair of seagulls flew overhead, high in the sky. But nothing else moved.

Tim stared at the remnants of his rented bicycle. Spokes pointed in every direction. The wheels were buckled and one tyre had been torn to shreds.

Tim decided to abandon it. He didn't even bother fastening the lock. No one was going to steal such a mangled wreck. Somehow, he would have to find enough money to reimburse Dino, the bike-rental man in Central Park, and buy back his own passport.

Tim felt nervous, but he knew what he had to do next. Get inside Doctor Wiener's factory. Find the Golden Dachshund. And steal it back.

He glanced at Grk, who was lying on the pavement, licking his paws. 'Let's go,' said Tim, clapping his hands. 'Come on, let's go!'

Grk glanced at Tim for a second, then returned to licking his paws.

Tim said, 'You're angry with me, aren't you?'

This time, Grk didn't even bother looking up. He just licked his paws as if Tim wasn't even there.

'There's no point being angry with me,' said Tim. 'I'm hungry too. And thirsty. You know what? I don't like it here either. But it's not going to get any better if you pretend to ignore me.'

Grk licked his paws as if they were the most delicious delicacies that he had ever encountered.

Tim said, 'Do you want to come with me? Or do you just want to lie on the pavement?'

Grk kept licking.

'Fine,' said Tim. 'Be like that.'

He turned his back on Grk and started walking.

Tim walked slowly to the end of the street. With every step that he took, something inside him wanted to look back and check if he was being followed by Grk, but he managed to resist the impulse.

He turned the corner and found himself opposite the gate that led into Doctor Wiener's factory.

Now, finally, Tim looked back. But there was no sign of Grk.

Fine, thought Tim. I don't care. If he wants to sulk, let him sulk.

Tim stared at the big black gate. It looked solid and impregnable. Six CCTV cameras pointed in different directions, staring up and down the street.

On the other side of the wall, the factory rose into the sky. The windowless walls were tall and gloomy. Dark smoke curled from the tall chimneys.

Staring at the factory, Tim felt extremely small and completely helpless. He couldn't imagine how to get past the big black gate. And even if he managed to break into the factory, he had no idea what to do next.

Tim wished he was someone else. A spy or a superhero. If only he had a few useful gadgets. Or X-ray vision. Or amazing strength. But he was just an ordinary twelve-year-old boy. He usually did okay at school, and once came equal top in a maths test, but he wasn't especially intelligent or knowledgeable. He could swim and run, but he wasn't especially fast or skilful. No one had trained him in spycraft or martial arts. He had no extraordinary powers.

He wondered if he had made a terrible mistake. Maybe Doctor Wiener had nothing to do with the theft of the Golden Dachshund. Maybe his theory was completely wrong. Maybe the dachshund had been stolen by the Mafia or a jewel thief or a guard who worked at the National Museum or some other burglar who just happened to be passing.

A chilly breeze blew along the street, scuffling some loose sheets of newspaper. Tim felt hungry and lonely and quite scared. He hadn't eaten or drunk anything for several hours. He was tired. His legs hurt. His elbows were bruised. His hands were covered in little cuts from the bike crash.

Perhaps I should just give up, thought Tim. I'm not a detective. I don't know where I am. I don't know what to do. And my belly is so empty, I might faint.

He took a deep breath and rubbed his face with his hand. This is crazy, he thought. I'm in the middle of nowhere, chasing a man that I know nothing about, and I'm starving to death. I've smashed a bicycle and lost my passport. And, worst of all, I'm not even on speaking terms with my best friend.

As soon as that thought entered Tim's mind, he realised there was only one thing that he needed to do.

Tim retraced his steps and went to find Grk. For a moment, just before he turned the corner, he worried that Grk might have decided to wander off in the other direction, searching for food or water or a new owner. Or perhaps he had been kidnapped. Or run over. Or attacked by a gang of stray dogs.

But to his relief, Tim saw that Grk was still lying on the pavement in exactly the same place, licking his paws in exactly the same way.

Grk must have heard Tim's footsteps, but he didn't bother lifting his head or wagging his tail. He concentrated on licking the dirt from his back feet.

Tim kneeled down on the pavement beside Grk. 'I'm really sorry,' Tim whispered. 'I'm an idiot. I didn't mean to shout at you.'

Grk continued licking. He seemed to have found something particularly fascinating embedded between the pads and claws of his right back foot. He dug his tongue into the crevice, pushing as hard as he could, trying to dislodge whatever it was.

'I know you're hungry,' said Tim. 'And I know you're thirsty. And I know you had to run all the way from Manhattan to Brooklyn. But that's not the worst thing, is it? The worst thing is that I was horrid to you.' Tim stroked Grk's soft ears. 'I'm really, really sorry. Will you forgive me?'

Grk lifted his head and turned to look at Tim. For a few moments, they stared into one another's eyes. Then Grk stretched his neck, extended his little pink tongue and licked Tim's hand.

'Thank you,' said Tim. He tickled Grk's ears.

They were friends again.

Together, Tim and Grk strolled to the end of the road. They were hungry and thirsty and tired, but none of that mattered. Together, they were going to discover if Doctor Wiener had stolen the Golden Dachshund. And if he had, they were going to steal it back again.

They stood opposite the big black gate for about ten minutes. During that time, the gate opened twice, once to let a white van in, and once to let a white van out. When the gate was open, Tim wondered whether it might be possible to sneak inside, hidden from the guards and the cameras behind one of the white vans, but he realised that there wasn't much hope. With (at least) three security guards and (at least) six CCTV cameras, the factory was protected like a fortress.

But sometimes fortresses have unguarded entrances. Usually at the back. Tim decided to walk around the perimeter of Doctor Wiener's factory, following the high wall, searching for... Well, until he found it, he wouldn't know exactly what he was searching for. But an unlocked door would be perfect. Or a fence with a hole that a boy and a dog could sneak through.

They walked quickly around the factory. They passed three locked iron gates and two locked metal doors, all bearing large signs which said PRIVATE PROPERTY and KEEP OUT and GUARD DOGS ON PATROL in big black letters.

A little further round the factory's perimeter, Tim did

discover a large gap in the wall, but he couldn't climb through it. The gap had been barricaded by a section of wire netting, ten feet tall, topped with spiky metal spears which looked extremely painful.

Tim peered through the fence. On the other side, he could see a building site. Cranes and diggers and trucks were parked beside a series of trenches. Nearby, there were some old buildings which had been half-demolished.

They were digging the foundations for a new building, Tim decided. Maybe even a new factory. The hot dog business must be getting even bigger.

After about fifteen minutes, Tim and Grk found themselves back where they started, standing opposite the gate that led into Doctor Wiener's factory.

Not knowing what else to do, Tim sat down in a shadowy doorway. If he wanted to spy on the factory, this was the perfect place to sit. He was hidden in the shadows, but he could watch the gate and see whoever went in and came out.

Grk walked in a circle three times, lay down at Tim's feet and immediately fell asleep.

Chapter 15

Every few minutes, the gate opened. Vehicles drove in and out. Most were white vans just like the one that Tim had followed. They must have been delivering supplies of sausages, buns, onions, mustard and ketchup to Doctor Wiener's hot dog stalls all around New York.

But one of the vehicles was very different.

After Tim had been sitting in the doorway for about half an hour, a long white limousine drove down the street and stopped opposite the big black gate. Slowly, the gate slid open.

The limo drove through the gate, then stopped opposite the hut where the security guards were sitting. The limo's back window opened. Someone leaned forward and spoke to the security guards, wagging a finger at them, telling them off.

Tim caught a brief glimpse of the person inside the limo. He couldn't see very much – the limo was on the other side of the street, and the face was partly hidden – but he glimpsed plump red cheeks and a blond moustache and a fat hand. He remembered exactly where he had last seen those cheeks, that moustache and that hand.

So, thought Tim, Doctor Wiener has come to inspect his factory. Perhaps he has even brought the Golden Dachshund with him.

The limo drove on and the gate swung shut.

Overhead, there was no sign of the sun in the murky sky. It would be dark soon.

Tim sat in the doorway and wondered what to do next. There was no way that he could sneak inside the factory. The walls were too high to climb. Although the gates opened every few minutes to let cars and vans in and out, the guards and cameras would have seen any intruders who took advantage of the opening.

So what was he going to do?

He had no money. He and Grk hadn't eaten since breakfast. They were stuck in the middle of nowhere with no way of getting out. Things were looking hopeless.

Just as Tim was beginning to despair, he heard a strange sound.

He cocked his head and listened. Yes, there it was again. He could hear music. And singing. It was coming from behind him. On the other side of the door.

Tim decided to investigate. He turned the handle. The door opened. It wasn't locked. He stepped inside, followed by Grk, and walked slowly down the hallway. Behind them, the door swung shut.

The corridor was lit by a single bulb. Tim could see a flight of wooden stairs leading upwards and two closed doors. He opened the first door and found a small cupboard, packed with brooms, buckets and cleaning materials.

He closed the first door and opened the second. He

found himself in a long room with a varnished wooden floor. At this end of the room, two men were lying on the floor and a woman was sitting on a plastic chair, reading a book. Down at the far end of the room, a small group of people were clustered around an upright piano. The pianist had pink hair. A drummer squatted on the floor with two bongo drums. All the singers wore black T-shirts and blue jeans. They had bare feet. They were swinging gently from side to side, clicking their fingers and clapping their hands as they sang.

> 'Don't get me a shirt! Don't buy me a tie!
> I don't need another pair of socks!
> All I want for Christmas is a brand new car,
> A Mustang or a Caddy or a Ford.'

Suddenly, a short man with lots of curly black hair stamped his foot on the floor and shouted, 'No!'

The singers stopped singing. The pianist and the drummer stopped playing. All of them stared at the curly-haired man.

He said, 'You have to put the accent on "car"! On "car"! How many times do I have to tell you?' No one responded. The curly-haired man shook his head. 'Okay, come on. Once more. And this time, please, put the accent on "car".' He nodded to the pianist, who immediately started playing the tune. The singers joined in, followed by the drummer.

Along the near wall, a few feet from Tim, there was a line of plastic chairs. A woman was sitting on one of the chairs. She grinned at Tim. 'Hiya,' she whispered.

'Hello,' said Tim.

The woman was about twenty-five years old and very pretty. She had brown hair, green eyes and perfect teeth. She beckoned at Tim. 'Come here,' she whispered. 'Sit down.'

Not knowing what else to do, Tim walked over to her and sat down. Grk padded after him, then lay at his feet.

'They'll be finished soon,' whispered the woman. 'You can wait here with me.'

'Okay,' said Tim.

The actors performed the song again and again, accompanied by the drummer and the pianist. The curly-haired director never seemed to be happy with what they were doing. Every few seconds, he clapped his hands, ordering them to stop. 'No, no, no,' he said. 'Not like that. Like this.' He sang a phrase or a word himself, then put his hands on his hips and stared at the actors. 'Do you get it? Do you understand the difference? Good. Then let's take it again from the top. Geraldine, please, from the top.'

Tim glanced at the woman sitting beside him. She smiled and whispered, 'Who's your mom?'

Tim said, 'What?'

'Is it Louisa? Are you Louisa's son?'

'No,' said Tim.

The woman pointed at the group of actors. 'Then which of them is your mom? Or your dad? Who have you come to meet?'

91

'No one,' said Tim.

'Then what are you doing here?'

'Nothing,' said Tim. 'I'm just sitting.'

The woman stared at him. Slowly, a smile spread across her face. 'Just sitting,' she said. 'That's a good answer. I like it. I guess that's what I'm doing too.' She nodded, still smiling. 'Hey, you have a nice accent. Are you British?'

Tim nodded. 'I'm from London.'

'That's cool,' said the woman. 'What are you doing in Brooklyn?'

'I'm a tourist.'

'Here? In Brooklyn? What's wrong with the Empire State Building?'

'I want to see the real New York,' said Tim. 'Not just the tourist sites.'

'It's certainly real round here. A bit too real, I'd say.' The woman twisted her head from side to side, then stretched her arms into the air.

Tim gestured at the room. 'Do you all live here?'

'No, no, no. We're rehearsing.' The woman pointed at the other men and women standing at the other end of the room. 'We're actors. Can't you tell by looking at us?'

Tim stared the men and women, then shook his head. 'No,' he said. 'They just look like normal people.'

The woman laughed. 'They might look like that,' she said. 'But they're not.' She sighed. 'Let me ask you something. Why would anyone in their right mind become an actor?'

'I don't know,' said Tim.

'You know what actors do all day? They wait. That's why so many of them work as waiters. Practice makes perfect. I've been waiting here since ten o'clock this morning.' She glanced at the pink watch on her wrist. 'And now it's almost six. What have I done? Nothing. I learn my lines. I warm up. I'm ready. And what happens? Nothing. I've just been waiting for something to happen.' She looked at Tim. 'You don't want to be an actor, do you?'

'I've never really thought about it,' said Tim.

'Well, let me give you a piece of advice. Don't.' The woman shook her head again. 'You want my advice, be something that earns a lot of money. A banker. An accountant. A dentist. My brother's a dentist. Gosh, his life is boring. But at least he earns a lot of money.' She extended her slim hand. 'I'm Smith, by the way.'

Tim gingerly took her hand. 'Hello, Smith,' he said. 'My name's Timothy Malt. But everyone calls me Tim.'

Smith said, 'Nice to meet you, Tim.' She vigorously shook his hand. 'And who's this?' She pointed at Grk.

'That's Grk.'

'Hi, Grk,' said Smith.

Grk opened one eye, looked at Smith for a moment, then closed his eye again and went back to sleep.

'He's not very friendly,' said Smith.

'He's tired,' said Tim. 'And hungry. He hasn't eaten all day.'

'That's tough,' said Smith.

They sat in silence for a second. Then Tim said,

93

'Smith. That's an interesting name.'

'Thanks,' said Smith.

'Were you, um... Were you called Smith by your parents?'

'That's a very personal question,' said Smith. 'I thought the British were supposed to be uptight.'

'Oh, I am uptight,' said Tim. 'But I'm also interested. Why did they call you "Smith"?'

'If you really want to know, my name is Janet. I was christened Janet Mocetta. But who wants to be called Janet Mocetta? So I changed it.'

Tim said, 'To Smith?'

'You don't like Smith?'

'I like it a lot,' said Tim.

'Good,' said Smith. 'I like Tim too. And Grk. You both have very nice names. In fact, we all have nice names.'

At that moment, the director stamped his foot on the floor again, and shouted, 'Stop! Stop! Stop, stop, stop!' When everyone stopped singing, the director said, 'I've had enough. This is ridiculous. Are you stupid? Are you deaf? Are you deliberately ignoring me?'

None of the actors replied. Nor did the drummer or the pianist.

'Very well,' said the director. 'Let's have a break. Back here in fifteen minutes, please.' He walked to the far end of the room and lay down on the floor.

The pianist closed the lid of the piano. The drummer pushed away his drums and stood up. Most of the actors hurried towards the door, heading out into the street to get some fresh air.

Smith gathered her things. 'Let's go outside,' she said. 'No point staying here on a break. Might as well get some fresh air. Come and meet the others.'

Tim looked at Smith. She had a nice face. He thought he could trust her. He said, 'Can I ask you something?'

'Sure,' said Smith.

'I want to get into that factory across the road. The factory that produces Doctor Wiener's hot dogs. Do you know how I might get inside?'

Smith said, 'Why do you want to go in there?'

Tim bit his fingernail, trying to think of a good answer. 'You know I said Grk hasn't eaten all day? Well, I haven't either. And I'd really love a hot dog.'

Smith grinned. 'Doctor Wiener does make good hot dogs,' she said. 'They're juicy and meaty and everything you could possibly want from a hot dog. Of course, I don't eat them.'

Tim said, 'You don't eat them?'

'No, no, no, I never eat them,' said Smith.

'Why not?'

'I'm on a diet,' said Smith. 'No hot dogs for me.' She smiled at Tim. 'But if you and your doggie want one, then maybe I'd have one too. Just to keep you company.'

She explained that Doctor Wiener's factory had a hot dog stand in its cafeteria. Anyone who worked at the factory got two hot dogs for a dollar, plus as much ketchup, mustard and onions as they could eat. It was the best bargain in Brooklyn.

Only workers were allowed inside the factory. So if you managed to sneak through the gates, everyone

95

would assume you were a worker, and you could buy two hot dogs for a dollar too.

'That sounds great,' said Tim. 'But how do you get inside? How do you get past the gate and the cameras and the guards?'

'With a smile,' said Smith.

'A smile?'

Smith nodded. 'Anything is possible with a smile.'

Chapter 16

Smith strolled out of the rehearsal room, followed by Tim and Grk. In the street, several actors were standing around, chatting and laughing. Some of them were smoking cigarettes and others were drinking from little bottles of water.

Smith walked over to the group and asked if anyone wanted a hot dog. Two people said yes, giving complicated instructions about exactly what quantities of ketchup, mustard and onions they preferred. They wanted to give Smith some money, but she waved it away, saying, 'No, no, I'm buying. You can get the next one. Hey, by the way, let me introduce my new friends. This is Tim and that's Grk.'

The actors smiled and waved and said a chorus of hellos.

Tim said, 'Hi.'

Grk said nothing, but he did wag his tail a couple of times.

'Let's go,' said Smith, winking at her fellow actors and putting her arm round Tim's shoulders. 'Hot dog time.'

Tim, Grk and Smith strolled across the street. When they reached the big black gate, Smith waved at the nearest CCTV camera.

Slowly, the gate swung open. Smith walked inside, followed by Tim and Grk.

Beside the gate, there was a small hut where the security guards sat, checking the identities of everyone who entered or left the factory. The security guards were drinking coffee and watching a game of American Football on the TV. The sound was turned down. One of the guards leaned out of the window and winked at Smith. 'Hello, beautiful,' he said.

'Hiya,' replied Smith with a big beaming smile which would have charmed any man on the planet, and most of the women too. She pointed through the window at the TV. 'Who's winning?'

'The Jets. Of course.'

'Go Jets! Go Jets! Go Jets!' chanted Smith with another of her dazzling smiles. 'And how's life been treating you?'

'Not bad, not bad,' said the security guard. 'You?'

'Yeah, okay.'

'How's the acting? Learnt your lines yet?'

'I know them back to front,' said Smith. 'We've only got one more week here. Then the rehearsals are over and we're on stage.'

'I'm still waiting for my tickets.'

'You'll get them,' said Smith. 'I promise.' She grinned again, giving the guard yet another dazzling smile, then pointed at Tim. 'Hey, this is my friend from England. He's visiting Brooklyn. He wants to see the real New York. Can I buy him a hot dog?'

'Sure you can,' said the security guard, waving them through the gate. 'Enjoy!'

Smith, Tim and Grk hurried into the factory. Behind

them, the black gate swung shut and the security guard went back to his football game.

Smith whispered in Tim's ear, 'You see? All it takes is a smile.'

As they walked across the yard, Tim looked around, trying to spot the white limousine. He couldn't see it. By the far wall, men in blue dungarees were loading crates into the back of white vans. Several doors led into different sections of the factory. A strange smell hung in the air, halfway between boiled meat and petrol.

'This way,' said Smith. 'Follow me.'

They walked to the end of the yard, through a door, down a corridor and into a large cafeteria, packed with tables and chairs. A line of men in dungarees were queueing to buy coffee and hot dogs. Smith and Tim joined the queue.

Tim said, 'I don't have any money.'

'That's no problem,' said Smith. 'This is my treat. When I come to London, you can buy me a cup of tea and a scone.'

When they reached the front of the queue, Smith bought five hot dogs. She handed the first two to Tim. 'For you and Grk,' she said.

Tim stared at the hot dogs in his hands. The delectable scent of onions and sausage swirled around his nostrils. He would have been happy to stuff both hot dogs into his mouth and chomp them down without chewing.

Grk sat on the linoleum floor, his tail thumping, his eyes fixed on the hot dogs.

Tim put one of the hot dogs on the floor.

Grk ate it in two gulps, then licked his lips and sniffed the floor, checking for crumbs. Finding none, Grk stared at Tim's left hand, where the second hot dog sat, warm and delicious, waiting to be eaten.

'I could give it to you,' said Tim. 'Or I could eat it myself.'

Grk wagged his tail.

'Hmmm,' said Tim, unsure what to do.

He could feel the hot dog's warmth against his palm. The smell of ketchup and meat seemed even more intense than before. His stomach was probably emptier than it had ever been in his entire life and he was weak with hunger. Every muscle in his body, every drop of blood in his veins, every brain cell in his head, demanded that he grab the hot dog with both hands and stuff it in his mouth and swallow it down as fast as possible.

But something stopped him.

He looked into Grk's big, hungry eyes.

Tim remembered his quarrel with Grk. He remembered walking round the corner on his own, leaving Grk in the street, licking his paws. He remembered standing opposite the factory's gates, feeling cold and frightened and horribly alone. Finally, he remembered going back to Grk, begging for forgiveness, and eventually being forgiven.

Tim knelt beside Grk. He whispered, 'This is because I was such an idiot. When I said things I didn't mean. Okay?' He put the hot dog on the floor.

Grk lunged forward with his mouth open, as if he had

to catch the hot dog before it had a chance to run away. He swallowed it down in two quick gulps.

Smith was holding three hot dogs, one for herself and two for her friends. 'We'd better hurry back,' she said. 'I have to deliver these before they get cold. Nothing worse than a cold hot dog, right?'

Together, the three of them walked out of the cafeteria and down the corridor. Before they reached the yard, they passed a doorway. Just at that moment, the door opened and two men in blue dungarees came out, laughing and talking. Behind the two men, Tim glimpsed a long, white corridor, lined with doors. That must be the main part of the factory. If you went down that corridor, you would probably find the offices of everyone who worked here, including Doctor Wiener.

Tim gestured at the doorway. 'I'm just going to have a look around. You go and deliver the hot dogs. I'll be out soon.'

Smith shook her head slowly from side to side. 'That's not such a good idea, Tim. I know you want to see the real New York, but this place isn't for tourists. How about a nice trip on the Staten Island Ferry?'

'I've been on the Staten Island Ferry,' said Tim. He opened the door. 'Don't worry about me, I'm old enough to look after myself. Thanks very much for the hot dogs.' He hurried through the doorway, followed by Grk.

Smith didn't like leaving Tim alone in the factory, but she knew that she couldn't tell him what to do. He wasn't her brother or her son. There was no reason that she should feel responsible for him. Oh well, she thought. Maybe he really is old enough to look after himself. Carrying her hot dogs, she headed back to the yard.

Tim and Grk found themselves in a long corridor with doors on either side.

They walked to the end of the corridor, then turned the corner.

Two men in blue dungarees were walking towards him. Tim felt a jolt of fear. He told himself to be brave. As the two men approached, he smiled at them and said in a casual voice, 'I'm sorry, I seem to be lost. Which way is Doctor Wiener's office?'

'You are lost,' said one of the men.

The other man said, 'You want me to call security? They'll take you straight there.'

'No, no, I'll be fine,' said Tim. 'Just tell me which direction to go.'

The two men were surprised, but did as he asked. They told him to turn left, then right, then left again, walk to the end, take the second right followed by the third left, and he would find himself at the entrance to the main office block. 'When you get there,' said one of the men, 'talk to the receptionist. Her name is Ruby. She's blonde.'

'And very cute,' added the other man.

'She's certainly cute,' said the first man. 'She'll tell Doctor Wiener you've arrived.'

Tim thanked the two men and hurried along the corridor, trying to remember their directions. He turned left, then right, then left again. He walked to the end of the corridor, turned right, then left, and found himself in yet another corridor. He could see three identical blue doors.

The first door led to a laboratory where men in white coats were hunched over test tubes and bunsen burners. Tim quickly shut the door and opened the next one. It led to yet another long white corridor lined with blue doors. That was no good. He opened the third door and found an office where six women in black suits were working at computers. None of them looked like a cute, blonde receptionist called Ruby.

Tim realised that he must have taken a wrong turning. The best thing to do, he decided, was retrace his steps, return to where he had started, and begin again.

Followed by Grk, Tim walked quickly down the corridor, turned right, went through a door, walked down two more corridors, turned left, stared ahead, stared behind, and came to the indisputable conclusion that he was completely and utterly lost.

At that moment, he heard a voice which said, 'Who are you?'

Tim and Grk turned round.

At the other end of the corridor, a tall man in a long white coat was staring at them. 'What are you doing here?'

'Looking for Ruby,' said Tim.

The man in the white coat shook his head. 'Ruby? Who's Ruby?'

'You know,' said Tim. 'Ruby. She's blonde. And very cute.'

'I don't know anyone called Ruby,' said the man in the white coat. 'Ruby who? Which department?'

'Don't worry,' said Tim. 'I'll be fine. I'll just go this way.' He smiled, and turned round, and started walking briskly away from the man in the white coat.

'Hey! Stop!'

Tim stopped and turned round. 'Yes?'

The man in the white coat pointed at Grk. 'What's that dog doing in here? Don't you know this is a restricted area?'

'Ruby said we could bring him here,' said Tim.

The man in the white coat shook his head. 'Well, Ruby is wrong. I think you'd better come with me. Come on.' He beckoned. 'I'll take you to security. They'll find Ruby.'

Tim stared at the man in the white coat. He knew there was only one thing he could possibly do. So he did it. He turned and ran as fast as he could in the opposite direction. Grk ran with him.

'Stop!' shouted the man in the white coat. 'Stop right there!'

But Tim and Grk had no intention of stopping. They sprinted down the corridor and took the first exit that they found.

The man in the white coat didn't follow them. He opened the nearest blue door and found the intercom fixed to the wall. There was a silver button under the intercom. He pressed it. 'Security,' he said into the intercom. 'I'm on level one, corridor three, and we have intruders. Repeat, we have intruders.'

Chapter 17

Have you ever been lost in a hot dog factory? As Tim quickly discovered, it's not much different to being lost anywhere else. You don't know where you are, you're not entirely sure how you got there and you have absolutely no idea how to get out.

Of course, if you're worried that a man in a white coat is chasing you, being lost is even worse. You can't stop and ask anyone for directions. You can't hang around in the same place, hoping someone friendly might come along and help you. You can't even try to retrace your steps, walking slowly back along the way that you came. All you can do is run as fast as possible until you find a good place to hide.

So that's what Tim did. He ran as fast as he could, searching for good places to hide, and Grk ran alongside him.

They ran past door after door, but Tim didn't go through a single one, knowing that he would just get trapped in an office or a laboratory.

Halfway down the corridor, Tim stopped. He glanced both ways. He couldn't see anyone, but he could hear footsteps and voices. He leaned down and unclasped the lead from Grk's collar. It was much easier for both of them to run if they weren't attached to each other.

There was a door opposite them. It opened and a

woman in a white coat stepped out. She said, 'Who are you?'

Tim wanted to say something clever or funny in response, but he couldn't think of anything funny or clever to say. So he ran. Grk ran after him.

The woman shouted, 'Stop!'

Tim and Grk didn't even pause.

The woman darted out of her office and sprinted after them, shouting at the top of her voice, 'Stop! You there, stop!' She must have been one of those women who goes jogging every morning before work, because she could run extremely fast.

I should go jogging every morning before school, thought Tim. Then I wouldn't get into trouble like this.

Of course, he wouldn't have got into trouble at all if he hadn't broken into a hot dog factory and sneaked down corridors that were clearly marked as private property. But that's a different matter.

Tim and Grk reached another, larger corridor. They could turn left or right. Tim glanced each way. On his left, he could see a security guard, dressed in a black uniform, running towards him, pointing and shouting. Tim turned right and sprinted along the corridor. Grk ran after him.

Tim glanced over his shoulder. The security guard was only a few feet away. The woman was just a few feet behind the security guard.

Drawing on his deepest reserves of energy, Tim put on an extra burst of speed and sprinted to the end of the corridor. Grk sped alongside him. Together, they turned the corner and came face to face with yet another man in a white coat. The factory was full of them. Doctor Wiener must have got a cheap deal on a lorryload of white coats.

This particular white-coated man was carrying a hundred test tubes on a silver tray. The test tubes were filled with liquids of all different colours – red, white, green, blue – and the man was carrying them with great care, making sure that he didn't spill a single drop.

Tim dodged round him. Grk ran between his legs. The man in the white coat blinked and said, 'What do you think you're...'

But before the man in the white coat could finish his sentence, the security guard tore round the corner and smacked straight into him. The force knocked both of them to the ground and sent the tray flying into the air. Test tubes went everywhere. Glass tinkled and shattered. The white walls and the floor and both men's clothes were splashed with multi-coloured liquid.

The man in the not-so-white-any-longer coat looked at the liquid and the walls and the glass and the security guard, and said, 'You...'

But before he could finish his sentence, or even really start it, the woman in the white coat sprinted round the corner. She tripped over the security guard's out-stretched leg and toppled forwards, waving her arms. The man in the coat-that-had-once-been-white didn't have time to move. She fell on top of him. Their heads cracked together and both of them slumped backwards, knocked unconscious.

Chapter 18

The factory had a very strict routine for dealing with intruders.

As soon as the Chief of Security received a message saying that an intruder had entered the factory, he alerted his men, sending squads to every exit. He ordered that the gates should be barred, letting no one in and no one out. He broadcast a message offering a reward of five hundred dollars to whoever caught the intruder.

Dr Wiener paid his workers very badly. In a week, most of them earned less than five hundred dollars. So the reward was a lot of money. All around the factory, ears lifted and eyes sharpened. People peered into dark corners and opened creaking doors, searching for the intruder, hoping to earn five hundred dollars.

The Chief of Security organised the hunt from his control room, where he had fifty screens connected to cameras in every part of the factory.

Doctor Wiener stood beside him. They stared at the fifty screens. They could see every corridor, every laboratory, every office and every section of the machinery. None of the screens showed any sign of an intruder.

'I don't understand it,' said Doctor Wiener. 'Where is he?'

'He must be somewhere,' replied the Chief of Security.

'I know he must be somewhere. Everyone has to be somewhere. That's physics. But the question is – where?'

'My men are combing every inch of this place,' said the Chief of Security. 'Whoever he is, and wherever he is, we'll find him soon.'

'You'd better,' said Dr Wiener.

Together, the two men stared at the screens, searching for the intruder.

Chapter 19

Tim kept running. Behind him, he heard smashes and shouts, but he didn't turn round to see what had happened. He was panting heavily, and his legs hurt, but he dared not pause for a rest.

The air was thick with the stench of boiling meat. There was a noise like revving engines, as if several huge trucks were driving at full speed up a steep slope.

Tim wondered whether it was better to run or hide. He couldn't keep running forever. But he didn't have anywhere to hide.

He decided to keep running until he found somewhere to hide.

The corridor ended at a pair of double doors. Tim pushed them open and hurried through. He found himself in the heart of the factory, staring at the machines which produced thousands of sausages every day. Wherever he looked, he could see frothing cauldrons, filled with liquid. Huge blades stirred the cauldrons. Shiny levers pumped back and forth. Cogs spun. Springs pulled. Gears clanked. Steam whistled from the pipes and the hot scent of boiling sausage meat hung over everything. If you worked here, you would have to shower for fifteen minutes at the end of the day just to get the stench off your skin and out of your hair.

At one end of the long, high room, two vast tubes

poked out of the wall, filled with the basic ingredients for the sausages. These tubes spat their contents into four massive cauldrons, each as big as a caravan.

In the middle of the room, twelve thinner tubes dropped from the ceiling, bringing more ingredients and dropping salt and pepper and spices into the meat. Yet more tubes snaked out of the cauldrons and fed the spiced meat into machines which shaped and chopped and squidged and pumped and rolled. Finally, at the other end of the room, sausages were spat out, dropped onto a conveyer belt and sent into the next room to be cooked, smoked and packed in plastic boxes.

Elsewhere in the factory, other machines spurted ketchup, mustard, chopped onions and white buns into more plastic boxes. Finally, all these boxes would be packed into white vans, driven out of the factory and delivered to Doctor Wiener's stalls all around the city.

In the midst of all this pumping machinery, Tim could see a hundred men and women, dressed in white coats, wearing white caps on their heads, white gloves on their hands and white masks over their mouths.

Tim wondered what to do. Should he sneak back through the double doors and find a better escape route? Or should he try to hide somewhere in this vast room? Looking around, he saw gaps between the cauldrons, metal ladders leading to shadowy gangways and dark spaces behind the huge tubes. Any of them would make a good hiding place. He just had to choose one.

But it was already too late. One of the men working on the nearest cauldron had noticed Tim. With his white-gloved hand, he tugged his neighbour's sleeve. Both of them stared at Tim for a second, as if they couldn't believe what they were seeing, then shouted and pointed, alerting the other people nearby. As the news spread across the room, more and more people turned round. Gradually, one after another, the white-coated workers stopped what they were doing and gazed at the double doors, until every person in the room was staring at Tim and Grk.

For a moment, no one moved.

Then a hundred men and women in white coats ran towards Tim, yelling and waving their arms.

Chapter 20

'There he is,' said the Chief of Security. 'They've got him cornered.'

He pointed at one of the screens. It was displaying an image from a camera high in the factory's roof. The screen showed a group of men and women in white coats advancing on a little figure.

Doctor Wiener peered at the screen. He couldn't see any details. The resolution was too small. 'Enlarge it,' he said. 'I want to see this guy's face.'

The Chief of Security issued an order to one of his subordinates, who twiddled a switch. The camera zoomed in. The image grew larger, focusing on the top of the intruder's head.

'That's no good,' said Doctor Wiener. 'I still can't see his face. Let me see his face!'

'No problem,' said the Chief of Security. He turned to his subordinates. 'Do we have any other cameras in there?'

'Yes, sir.'

'Well, what are you waiting for? Move them! Focus them! Zoom in! We want to see this guy's face.'

Three security guards hunched over the camera controls, fiddling with switches and pulling levers. The screens flashed, showing a multitude of images. Cameras twisted and turned. Lenses zoomed and focused.

'That's it,' said the Chief of Security. 'Yes! Zoom! Zoom! Zoom!'

The three security guards turned more switches and clicked different levers. Now, every screen showed the same sight from a different angle, inspecting the intruder from above and below and ahead and behind. In silence, Doctor Wiener, the Chief of Security and the guards stared at forty images of the same person.

The Chief of Security was the first to speak. 'It's a kid,' he said. 'It's just a kid.'

The security guards laughed and shook their heads. All this fuss – just for a kid! An ordinary little kid.

But Doctor Wiener wasn't laughing. He walked forward and stared at the nearest screen, peering directly into the boy's face. 'I know him.'

'You know him?'

'I've seen him somewhere before,' said Doctor Wiener. 'But where?'

Chapter 21

What would you do if a hundred people in white coats were running towards you, yelling and waving their arms?

Would you? Really?

Well, I'm impressed.

That's not what I would do. And it's not what Tim did either.

He turned round and ran away as fast as he could. He pushed the double doors, then realised that running down the corridor wasn't such a good idea, because six security guards were already jogging towards him. Two of them held pistols. The other four were carrying black truncheons. 'Stop right there!' shouted one of the security guards, raising his pistol.

Tim jumped backwards, letting the double doors swing shut, and turned round.

In the last few seconds, the hundred men and women in white coats had got a lot closer. The nearest one was only about ten feet away.

'This way,' hissed Tim to Grk, and darted in the opposite direction, running down a flight of metal stairs. Grk followed him.

Behind them, more feet clattered down the stairs. Tim and Grk didn't turn around to see who owned the feet. They darted left, then right, running round a cauldron and dodging under a tube.

Tim could feel the cauldron's heat on his face. He tried not to lose his balance or skid on the floor. If he touched the hot metal, his skin would be fried like an egg in a pan.

He sprinted through the factory, darting between pipes, avoiding cogs and levers, until he found his way blocked by two broad-shouldered men in white coats.

He looked to his left. Another man was standing there.

He looked to his right. Three women blocked that route.

He turned round. Four more men filled the gap that he had come through. Others pushed behind them, straining forwards, trying to see over people's shoulders and catch a glimpse of the intruder.

Tim was surrounded. Every exit was blocked by a man or woman in a white coat, a white cap, a white mask and white gloves. There was no escape. He didn't know what to do next. Hoping for inspiration, he looked down at Grk.

Grk looked up at Tim and wagged his tail.

That was one of the great things about Grk. Even in the most desperate, dangerous and appalling situations, he still managed to remain cheerful.

But it's easy to be happy if you don't have a clue what's going on. Tim had a terrible premonition of what was going to happen next, so he couldn't possibly be cheerful. He had a horrible feeling that the men and women in white coats were now going to rush forward and grab him. They would hold his arms and legs in their white gloves. They would climb the nearest staircase and walk along the gangway until they were directly above the biggest cauldron. They would force him to look down. For a second or two, he would stare down at the steaming goo of sausage meat and spices. Then they would let go of his arms and legs, dropping him into the hot sludge. And they would throw Grk after him.

The men and women in white coats took a step towards Tim and Grk. Then they took another step. They were barely more than an arm's length away. One more step and they could grab him.

'Wait,' said Tim.

The men and women in white coats stared at him.

'Let's be sensible about this,' said Tim. 'What do you want? Why are you chasing me? I haven't done anything to you.'

Standing opposite Tim, there was a short man with frizzy hair and a dangly moustache which looked like a mouse's tail. He said, 'I'll tell you what I want. What I want is five hundred dollars. So come with me and let's claim the reward.'

'Reward,' said Tim. 'What reward?'

'The reward for finding you. Come on, let's get moving.'

'No way,' said another man. 'You're not getting five hundred dollars. I am!'

'You?' The man with the mouse-tail moustache laughed. 'Why should you get it? He's mine.'

'No,' said a third man. 'He's mine. I found him.'

'You didn't find him,' said a fourth man, who was taller and wider than any of these others. 'We all found

117

him. But I caught him.' He stepped forward and stood beside Tim. 'And anyone who thinks different is going to have to fight me for him.'

'I'll fight you,' said the man with the mouse-tail moustache. 'I'll knock you down with one hand tied behind my back.'

'Guys, guys, guys,' said a woman. 'Be reasonable. I've got three kids to feed. I need five hundred dollars more than you.'

'My mother's in hospital,' said someone else. 'And she don't have no medical insurance.'

'I'm half a year behind with my rent,' said another man. 'With five hundred bucks, I won't get evicted.'

The man standing beside Tim – the one who was taller and wider than anyone else – shook his head slowly from side to side. 'I'm very sorry about your mother and your kids and your eviction,' he said. 'But I have rent to pay and a wife to keep and two kids of my own. And this five hundred dollars is all mine. Get out the way.'

No one moved.

'Be like that,' said the tall, wide man. He grabbed Tim's collar and jerked him forward, pushing through the crowd, heading for the double doors. He didn't get far before someone else pushed him aside and lunged at Tim. Two more men jumped into the fray. Someone threw a punch. A woman screamed. A man started kicking anyone within range. Within seconds, a full-scale brawl had broken out, involving a hundred people, yelling and screaming, punching and kicking, trying to wrestle one another to the ground.

118

It didn't take Tim long to realise that he and Grk had been completely forgotten. The tall, wide man had released his collar in order to return a punch. No one had time or space to think about anything except defending themselves. Tim crouched down, grabbed Grk in his arms, and pushed through the crowd.

Avoiding the hail of boots and fists, he emerged on the other side of the crowd, dodged round a hot cauldron and glanced behind him. He wasn't being followed. Tim grinned. He dashed towards the staircase, planning his next move.

He would sprint down the corridor, he decided, and get as far away as possible from these lunatics. Then he would find a good hiding place. He would stay there for a few hours, waiting for the fuss to die down.

Grinning to himself, delighted with the sound of his new plan, he put Grk on the floor and attached the lead to his collar. Together, they climbed the stairs and reached the double doors.

Two security guards were standing beside the doors. One of them pointed a pistol at Tim. 'You'd better come with us, kid.'

Chapter 22

They walked for about ten minutes through a series of unmemorable corridors. Tim looked for opportunities to escape, but there were none. One of the guards always stayed right behind him and one in front. Every now and then, the guard behind nudged his pistol into the middle of Tim's back, reminding him not to do anything stupid.

They emerged into the open air, crossed a yard and reached a shabby office block. On the ground floor, there was a reception area with a few chairs and a muddy-coloured carpet. Posters on the walls described the nutritional benefits of eating hot dogs.

A blonde woman sat behind a long desk, answering the telephone and taking the names of visitors. She nodded to the two guards. 'He's waiting for you,' she said.

'Thanks,' said the guard. 'Come on, kid. This way.'

Tim smiled at the blonde woman and said, 'Hi, Ruby.'

She stared at him, her eyes wide with surprise. 'How do you know my name?'

Before Tim could reply, the security guard pushed him past the desk. 'Move it, kid. Let's go.' Tim stumbled towards the lift, pulling Grk with him, and the two security guards followed.

Ruby stared after them, trying to remember where she might have seen that boy before. Now she came to think about it, he did look a little like Mrs Barton's nephew, the one who was so good at Scrabble. Had she met him last year at Thanksgiving?

The two security guards followed Tim and Grk into the lift. One of them pressed the button for the third floor. The door shut and the lift went up.

They emerged on the third floor, stepping from the lift onto a lush cream-coloured carpet. Vases of flowers stood at regular intervals along the hallway. Interesting pictures hung on the walls. It looked more like a hotel than a factory.

'This way,' said the security guard, nudging Tim down the corridor. They walked for a couple of minutes, then reached a white door. The guard knocked twice.

'Come in,' said a woman's voice.

They went inside. A pretty blonde woman was sitting behind a desk. She smiled. 'Go right in, please.'

They walked through the open door into Doctor Wiener's office. Doctor Wiener was standing in the middle of the room, waiting for them. He was wearing the same clothes as the previous time that Tim had seen him: a white suit, white socks and white shoes. His face was red and his hair was blond.

At the other end of the room, there was a huge desk, piled with pieces of paper, and a big black leather chair.

Ten framed certificates hung on the left-hand wall. They were the prizes that Doctor Wiener's hot dogs had won. On the right-hand wall, there was an enormous map of New York, covered in red dots, showing the locations of Doctor Wiener's hot dog stalls. Two huge framed photographs hung on the far wall, one of Doctor Wiener himself and another of a hot dog, smothered in mustard.

No one spoke. No one moved. The only noise came from Grk, who was sniffing the carpet, trying to trace the origin of an interesting scent.

Doctor Wiener was the first to break the silence. He lifted his arm and pointed a podgy finger at Tim. 'Don't I know you? Have we met?'

'I don't think so,' said Tim.

Doctor Wiener took a long look at Tim, then a long look at Grk, and finally shrugged his shoulders. He was sure that he'd seen the two of them somewhere before, but he couldn't remember where or when. 'What's your name?'

'Timothy Malt. But everyone calls me Tim.'

'And what are you doing in my hot dog factory?'

'I was hungry,' said Tim. 'I wanted a hot dog.'

Doctor Wiener couldn't help smiling. 'You like my hot dogs?'

'I love them,' said Tim. 'They're the best hot dogs I've ever eaten. They're famous in England. Before I came to New York, people said to me, you have to eat one of Doctor Wiener's hot dogs.'

'Really?' Doctor Wiener's smile broadened. 'People are talking about my hot dogs in England?'

'Oh, yes,' said Tim. 'Everyone's talking about them. That's why I came to your factory. Because I wanted to eat the best hot dogs in the United States.'

Doctor Wiener suddenly looked suspicious. He peered through his piggy eyes at Tim and Grk. 'So how did you get inside? This factory is a fortress. No one comes in, no one goes out, without me knowing about it.'

'I sneaked into the back of a white van,' said Tim. 'It was delivering hot dogs in Greenwich Village. The driver left the door open so I got inside. When it drove through the gates, I got out. No one stopped me.'

Doctor Wiener nodded. He made a mental note to discover which driver had done the Greenwich Village run today and fire him immediately. 'You're a clever kid,' said Doctor Wiener. 'And did you have a hot dog yet?'

'No, not yet,' said Tim.

Doctor Wiener clicked his fingers at the two security guards. 'Go downstairs, boys. Fetch a couple of hot dogs. One for the kid and one for the dog. A dog for the dog! Heh-heh-heh.' Doctor Wiener chuckled at his own pun. 'A dog for the dog, eh? Heh-heh-heh-heh.'

The guards laughed too. It's always a good idea to laugh at your boss's jokes.

Tim smiled. 'Thank you. That's very kind.'

'Oh, it's my pleasure.' Doctor Wiener waved his hand at the guards. 'Go on, both of you. Fetch the hot dogs. Bring them back here. And bring one for me too.'

'Sure, boss,' said one of the guards.

The other guard said, 'What about the kid? What shall we do with him?'

'The kid stays here,' said Doctor Wiener. 'We're having a nice little conversation. Right, kid?'

'Right,' said Tim.

The guards nodded. They hurried out of the room and closed the door after them.

When they had gone, Doctor Wiener looked at Tim and said, 'Do you think I'm a complete idiot?'

Tim blinked. He was so surprised, he couldn't think of anything to say. He just stood there, shaking his head slowly from side to side.

Doctor Wiener said, 'You were at the opening of the exhibition at the National Museum. Squatting on the floor. With that mutt. And a little girl. Right?'

'That's right,' said Tim, realising that there was no point lying.

'And what are you doing here?'

'Looking for the Golden Dachshund.'

'Here? In my factory? Why?'

'Because you stole it,' said Tim.

Doctor Wiener didn't even try to deny it. He walked back to his desk, pressed a button and spoke into the intercom. 'Ruby? Could you ask Mr Bock to come up here, please. Right now. Thank you.'

Tim wondered who Mr Bock might be, and what he would do when he arrived.

'Sit down,' said Doctor Wiener, waving at the chairs on the other side of his desk. 'I can see there's no point playing games. You know everything, don't you?'

'Yes,' said Tim. He didn't know everything, of course. He knew almost nothing. But he suspected that bluffing was probably the best course of action.

'It's all King Jovan's fault,' said Doctor Wiener. 'I tried to buy that statue many times. I offered him a lot of money.

If he'd had the good sense to sell, none of this would have happened. But he's an old fool. Don't you think so?'

'I don't really know him,' said Tim.

'I can tell you, he's an old fool.'

'And why did you want the statue? To add to your art collection?'

Doctor Wiener smiled. A small, vicious smile with no trace of amusement or friendship. 'You are well-informed, aren't you? How do you know about my art collection?'

'Oh, I know a lot,' said Tim. 'You collect paintings of dachshunds, don't you?'

'Not just paintings of dachshunds,' said Doctor Wiener. 'Sculptures of dachshunds. Pottery with dachshund decoration. Even a set of nineteenth-century silver knives with dachshunds carved on the handles. I have the finest collection of dachshund art in the country. Probably in the entire world.'

'And you were willing to do anything, absolutely anything, to get your hands on the Golden Dachshund. Weren't you?'

'There's been a hole in my collection for a long time,' said Doctor Wiener. 'A Golden-Dachshund-shaped hole. And now I've filled it.' Doctor Wiener chuckled. 'Heh-heh-heh.'

'And what about Colonel Zinfandel?'

'Colonel who?'

'Colonel Zinfandel.'

'Who's he?'

'The dictator who rules Stanislavia.'

'Oh, yeah. That guy. What about him?'

'Did he help you?'

'I never met the guy. Never even talked to him. Why would he help me?'

Tim shrugged his shoulders. 'I thought he might have done.'

'Well, he didn't.' Doctor Wiener smiled. 'This is all my own work.' He leaned back in the chair and rubbed his hands together. 'Listen, kid, tell me one thing. How did you find me?'

'Simple deduction,' said Tim. 'I looked at the facts and deduced the solution.'

Doctor Wiener nodded. 'That's extremely impressive. You must be a very smart kid. You really solved the mystery on your own? No one helped you?'

'Only Grk,' said Tim, not wanting to take all the credit for himself.

'Grk? What's Grk?'

'This is Grk,' said Tim, pointing at Grk.

'Oh. That's Grk.' Doctor Wiener nodded. 'I have to say, it's magnificent.' He clapped his hands together a few times as if he was applauding a wonderful perform-ance. 'You're alone. You came here. You solved the mystery. You caught me fair and square. You've done very well.'

'Thanks,' said Tim. Now he came to think about it, he was quite impressed too. Only twelve years old – and he had done better than the New York Police Department. Anyone would have been impressed by that.

'But you will have to explain one thing to me,' said

126

Doctor Wiener.

'I'll explain whatever you like,' said Tim. In his moment of triumph, he was willing to be generous. 'What do you want to know?'

'Right now, I'm planning to kill you. How exactly are you going to stop me?'

Tim blinked. His mouth opened, then closed again. Suddenly, he realised that he had been rather stupid. Brave, yes. Clever, certainly. Daring, undoubtedly. But also rather stupid. 'I called...' he stammered, desperately trying to think of a good lie. 'I've sent... There's a... The police will be here in five minutes.'

In response, Doctor Wiener just laughed. His fat belly wobbled. His cheeks went bright red. He chortled as if he had never heard anything so funny in his entire life. 'Heh-heh-heh-heh-heh-heh.'

While Doctor Wiener was laughing, the door opened. A tall, thin man in a black suit walked into the room. Although Tim had never previously seen his face, he recognised him instantly as the man from the National Museum. The shape of his body was extremely distinctive.

'Ah, Bock,' said Doctor Wiener. 'I'd like you to meet Tim.'

Bock slowly turned his head and looked down at Tim. 'Hello, Tim.'

'Hi,' said Tim in a nervous voice. There was something very frightening about Bock's face. He had a long nose, high cheekbones, and lips so thin that they barely existed. A scarlet scar ran from his left ear to his Adam's apple. Someone must have tried to cut his throat, but they only got halfway.

Doctor Wiener grabbed the desk and eased himself to his feet. Freed of his weight, the leather chair rocked back and forth. He hauled himself around the desk and smiled at Tim. 'It's been nice to meet you, kid. You're clever. You're cute. I wish we could stay friends. Sadly, we're never going to see one another again. In fact, no one is ever going to see you again.'

Tim wanted to be brave, but he couldn't. His courage had deserted him. He just felt frightened and lonely. He said, 'What are you going to do?'

'Kill you,' said Doctor Wiener.

'No, please,' said Tim. 'Are you going to drop us in the machines? And chop us up? And make us into sausages?'

Doctor Wiener stared at Tim. A grin spread slowly across his face. 'Why, you really are a clever kid. That's a great idea! Thank you so much for the suggestion.'

Tim felt sick with horror. Had he just made his own fate even worse?

Doctor Wiener giggled. 'Heh-heh-heh. Only joking. You really think I'd let my beautiful frankfurters be polluted by a little brat like you? You think I put real dogs in my hot dogs? No, no, kiddo. We'll just shoot you. And we'll shoot that nasty dog too. And then we'll throw your bodies in the East River.'

Tim said, 'Are you going to do it now?'

'I'm afraid not,' said Doctor Wiener. 'The last shift works till midnight. We'll have to wait till they go home.' He hauled his bulk across the room to the huge map of

New York. With his pudgy forefinger, he pointed at one of the red dots, just on the junction of 79th and Broadway. 'Until then,' said Doctor Wiener, 'you can wait on the building site. And don't bother screaming. No one will hear you.' He pressed the red dot. With a shuddering groan, the map slid sideways along the wall, revealing a dark passageway. 'Take him away,' said Doctor Wiener.

Bock put his hand in the middle of Tim's back and shoved him forwards. Tim stumbled into the passageway. Grk scurried after him. Bock walked behind them.

When they had gone, Doctor Wiener pressed the red dot again and the map slid shut.

Chapter 23

Tim and Grk walked down the dark passageway. Bock walked behind them. After about fifty paces, they reached a fork.

'Turn left,' said Bock.

They turned left, walked another fifty paces and found themselves beside a door.

'Open it,' said Bock.

Tim opened the door and stepped through the doorway. He was standing in a long, white corridor.

'Walk,' said Bock.

They walked down the corridor to another door. There were two heavy bolts on the outside. Bock pulled the bolts, opened the door and threw Tim inside.

'Don't move,' said Bock. He pulled a rope from his pocket.

Tim lay on the floor, his face pressed against the cold concrete.

The loud click of a turning key was followed by the heavy clunk of two bolts.

Grk hurried around the room, sniffing the walls, poking his nose into the corners, checking for good smells, hoping that one of the previous occupants might have left half a chicken sandwich or a slice of pizza.

The sound of footsteps dwindled down the length of the corridor and disappeared. Then there was silence.

Grk couldn't find any food in the room. So he came and lay down near Tim, and closed his eyes. A moment later, he was snoring.

Tim didn't move.

He couldn't move. His hands and feet were tied together.

But he could wriggle. And stretch.

Experimenting slowly, wriggling his arms, stretching his legs, he discovered that he could roll over and sit up.

He inspected his surroundings. He had been locked in a small, dingy room with dirty walls and a concrete floor. A single bulb dangled from the middle of the ceiling, switched off. The only light came through the window, the last lingering glow from the setting sun, but that wasn't much. Soon, darkness would fall and the room would be black.

Tim's wrists were tied behind his back. His ankles had been fastened together with the same rope, which had then been passed around his wrists, tethering his arms and legs together. He couldn't scratch his nose or rub his eyes.

Tim pulled his hands and his feet apart, trying to exert as much pressure as possible on the rope. It didn't budge. It just tightened, increasing the pressure on his wrists and ankles. If he pulled any more, the ropes would grip so tight that the blood would stop flowing to his fingers and toes.

No one knows I'm here, thought Tim. No one is going

to come and find me. No one will ever know what happened to me.

He tried to imagine what his parents would be doing now. Would they be thinking about him? Would they be worrying about him?

He thought about Max and Natascha. He wondered what Doctor Wiener might be planning. And he tried not to think about Bock.

But the more that he tried to avoid thinking about Bock, the more that his mind was flooded with memories of Bock's lean fingers and Bock's strong arms and Bock's cruel mouth and the scarlet scar that ran halfway across Bock's throat.

He shook his head. If he carried on thinking about Bock, he would go crazy.

He looked at Grk. 'Hey,' he said. 'Hey, Grk. Tell me something. How can you sleep at a time like this?'

Grk opened his eyes and stared at Tim for a few seconds. Then he shut his eyes again and went back to sleep.

'Thanks a lot,' said Tim. 'You're a big help.'

That time, Grk didn't even bother opening his eyes.

Tim wished that he could speak Dog. He'd like to know how Grk could stay so calm at a time like this.

He decided that, even if Grk didn't want to communicate with him, he was going to talk to Grk. If Grk didn't want to listen, he didn't have to listen.

'This is how I see our situation,' said Tim. 'It seems to me that things are pretty simple. Bock is going to come back at midnight. When he comes back, he's going to kill us. So we've got a few hours. What shall we do? Sleep? Or try to escape?'

Grk's answer was obvious. He would rather sleep.

'That's fine,' said Tim. 'You sleep. Leave me to do all the work.'

He rolled over and over on the floor, bashing every part of his body on the concrete, elbows and knees and shoulders and skull, causing himself a lot of pain, until he finally reached the wall. He lay there for a minute, waiting for the worst of the pain to throb away, then twisted his body round, using the bricks as a leverage. On the third attempt, he managed to squat in an upright position. Slowly, with his back pressed against the brickwork, he edged upwards. He wobbled forwards, then back again, but managed to stay steady.

He grinned. He'd done it. His ankles and wrists might have been tied together, but he had still managed to stand up.

Have you ever tried to stand up straight with your arms and legs tied together? It's not easy. And moving is a lot more difficult. You can't walk. You can't even take a pace. You can only hop.

Tim hopped. And hopped again. He wobbled, but managed to stay standing. With three or four more hops, he would be standing beside the window.

He hopped once more. Now, he could see through the window. The thick bars obscured his view, but he could distinguish a few shapes on the other side of the dirty glass. A yellow crane. A yellow truck. A cluster of metal poles stuck into the ground.

Tim remembered walking around the factory's perimeter and seeing a building site. That's where I am now, thought Tim. I must be locked in one of the old buildings. One that they haven't yet knocked down.

He tried to remember what else he had seen. People? No, the building site had been completely deserted. Guard dogs? No, there weren't even any dogs. He couldn't remember seeing anything apart from a few vehicles and the foundations of a new building.

He needed to get closer to the window. He hopped, then hopped again, and hopped once more. On the third hop, he missed his footing and toppled forwards. There was no way to protect himself. He couldn't raise his hands to cover his face. He just fell forwards and smacked into the floor, hitting first his knees, then his elbows and finally his head.

The agony was unbelievable. Tim felt as if he had broken half the bones in his body. His skin burned with pain.

He whimpered. Nothing had ever hurt so much. Tears formed in his eyes, and then he was sobbing. He didn't care if anyone heard him. He wept loudly and desperately.

Through his half-closed eyes, he saw a blurry splash of scarlet. He opened his eyes. There was a red spot on the concrete. He lifted his head. Blood and tears were dripping from his face.

His nose was bleeding.

There was nothing he could do. His hands were tied behind his back. He couldn't reach his nose to wipe away the blood. Nor could he check if any bones were broken. He just lay on the floor, helpless and immobile, crying quietly to himself. He hoped Bock would come for him soon. He wanted it to be over. He had had enough.

Chapter 24

Something pressed against Tim's face. He could feel softness and warmth.

Tim opened his eyes and found his vision blocked by a white bundle. As if the landscape had been covered in a thick snowfall.

He moved his head backwards. The whiteness was Grk, who had come to lie on the floor beside Tim's head.

'Hello,' whispered Tim.

Grk lifted his head and stared at Tim.

For a minute or two, they looked at one another.

Tim said, 'It's hopeless, isn't it?'

Grk just looked at him.

A tear eased out of Tim's eye and trickled slowly down his cheek.

'I don't want to die,' whispered Tim.

Grk said nothing.

Tim stared into Grk's big brown eyes. On the curve of Grk's pupil, he could see the reflection of his own face. But he could see something else too. Something that he couldn't really understand or even put into words. Something deep inside Grk's eye.

If you had asked Tim to describe what he had seen, he wouldn't have been able to tell you. But whatever it was, it made him feel stronger.

He whispered, 'We're not going to give up, are we?'

Grk opened his mouth, showing his tiny white pointed teeth, and barked twice. The noise echoed around the room.

Tim stared at him.

Very slowly, a smile spread across Tim's face. 'Oh, yes,' he whispered. 'That's it! You're a genius, Grk. You are a genius!'

Chapter 25

Grk needed a lot of persuasion. At first, he simply couldn't understand what Tim wanted him to do. Once he did understand, he didn't show any inclination to do it. He licked Tim's hands, and sniffed Tim's shoes, and lay on the floor, and wandered around the other end of the room, checking for food, although he had already checked every scrap of space in the room and must have known that there wasn't a crumb to be found.

Each time that Grk wandered off, Tim called him back again, and patiently begged him to help. It took at least an hour of begging and cajoling before Grk could finally be persuaded to start chewing on the rope.

But once he did start chewing, he chewed fast and efficiently, shredding the strands between his strong jaws. His teeth might have been small, but they were extremely sharp. While Grk gnawed, Tim wriggled his wrists, pushing and pulling, trying to snap the rope.

At first, Tim couldn't feel any difference. The rope bit into his wrists, pinching the skin and cutting off his circulation. His fingers ached from the lack of blood.

Minute by minute, Grk's teeth sawed through the strands. The rope loosened its grip. The knots slackened. The tight cords broke into threads. Tim strained with all his strength. He could feel his muscles aching. The pressure made his head hurt. His wrists throbbed. His arms begged for a rest. Ignoring all the separate pains in all the different parts of his body, Tim kept pulling and pulling and pulling until, with a suddenness that made him fall over backwards, the rope broke.

'Yes!' cried Tim. He jerked the rope and freed his right hand, then his left. 'Yes! Yes!' He flexed his fingers and shook his wrists and rolled his arms in their sockets.

Grk lay down, his tail thumping on the concrete, and waited to see what was going to happen next. He liked this game.

Now Tim's hands were free, the rest was easy. The rope had been tied tightly around his ankles, but his nimble fingers quickly undid the knots. He kicked the rope away, jumped to his feet and ran round the room three times, waving his arms in the air, taking great long leaps with his legs, getting the blood flowing through his limbs again.

Grk ran after him, barking joyfully.

'Sshhhh, we'd better keep the noise down,' whispered Tim.

He and Grk stood still, listening. What was that sound? Footsteps? Voices? No, just the wind. They hadn't been overheard by anyone.

Tim tried the door, tugging the handle. It was locked. He put his shoulder against the door and pushed with all his strength, but it didn't budge.

He walked to the window and peered through the dirty glass. Outside, night had fallen. The building site was dark and gloomy. Tim could just distinguish the silhouettes of a few large vehicles. There was a crane parked nearby. A little further away, there was a digger and three trucks. Nothing moved. There were no people to be seen.

Tim wrapped his hands around the thick iron bars and tried pulling them, then pushing them, but he couldn't even feel a wobble. Each bar was firmly embedded in the brickwork. A grown man with a crowbar might have knocked them out, but a boy with nothing but his fists couldn't do anything.

There were six horizontal bars and four vertical bars, forming a cage over the window. The gap between each bar was less than a foot. There was no way to squeeze through them. Tim's head might have fitted, but not his shoulders.

I'm trapped, thought Tim. My hands are free, and my legs are free, but I can't go anywhere. Undoing the rope hasn't helped me at all. I'm stuck in this room. I'm just going to have to wait here till Bock comes back and kills us.

What else could he do? The door was locked and bolted. The floor was concrete. The window was blocked by thick iron bars. He could break the glass and yell through the hole but no one would hear him except Doctor Wiener's workers.

An idea formed in his mind. It wasn't a particularly good idea. But it was the only idea that he had.

He walked over to the window and checked the size of the gaps between the bars. He turned round and looked at Grk.

Grk stared at Tim.

140

'You're going to have do something very difficult,' said Tim. 'You'll have to run to the other side of the factory. Break out of the gate. Find Smith. And bring her back here. Can you do that? Do you remember Smith? Yes? Smith! Smith! Remember Smith!'

Grk wagged his tail and barked excitedly.

'Good boy,' said Tim. 'You have to find Smith. And bring her here. Can you do that?'

Grk barked again. Perhaps he understood. Perhaps he didn't. There was no way of telling.

If there was anything else that Tim could have done, he would have done it. But there wasn't. This was his only chance. He couldn't get through the bars himself. Apart from Smith, there was no one else for miles around who would be able to help him.

Tim kneeled on the concrete and unlaced his shoe. He walked to the window, holding the shoe in his right hand. 'Get back,' he said. 'Go on! Get back!'

Grk retreated, looking surprised and a bit insulted. Why should he go away? What had he done wrong?

Tim lifted his right arm. With all his strength, he smashed the shoe against a windowpane. The glass fell out, dropping through the air and tinkling on the earth outside.

Using the shoe like a hammer, Tim knocked the rest of the glass from the pane. A chilly breeze blew through the gap. When the pane was completely clear, Tim put his shoe back on and clapped. 'Come here, boy. Come here!'

Grk ran to him.

Using both arms, Tim picked Grk off the ground. Tim

bent his head and nuzzled his face into Grk's fur. 'You have to save us,' he whispered. 'You have to find Smith.'

Grk opened his mouth and licked Tim's nose.

'That tickles,' said Tim.

Grk did it again.

Tim lifted Grk to the broken windowpane. Slowly and carefully, he eased Grk's paws and body past the last jagged scraps of smashed glass. Grk turned his head from side to side, sniffing the cold air and peering into the darkness. Tim stretched his arms to their full extent, then let go. With a surprised yelp, Grk plunged to the ground.

There was a thump, followed by a squeak.

Tim peered through the gap. Grk was lying on the ground, staring at him with an expression of profound shock. 'I'm sorry,' whispered Tim. 'Now, go! Find Smith! Go!'

Grk gingerly got to his feet. He sniffed his front paws. He sniffed his back paws. He wrinkled his nose and looked around, inspecting his surroundings.

'Smith,' hissed Tim.

Grk looked at Tim. His tail wagged.

'Oh, please,' whispered Tim, beginning to wonder if he could possibly communicate what he wanted. 'Go and find Smith.'

Grk's tail wagged even faster.

At that moment, Tim started to despair. 'SMITH,' he shouted, not caring who heard him. 'Find Smith! Find Smith! FIND SMITH!'

Grk put his head on one side and stared at Tim.

'Oh, no,' sighed Tim. 'You don't have any idea what I'm talking about, do you?'

At that moment, without any warning, Grk turned and ran across the building site.

For a few seconds, Tim could see him in the gloom, a white splash moving quickly across the dark earth. And then he was gone.

Chapter 26

Tim waited for a long time. He paced up and down the room, listening to his footsteps on the concrete. He peered through the broken pane, staring at the desolate building site, watching for signs of life, but seeing none. He paced. He stared. He paced some more.

At first, he was hopeful, even excited. He pictured Grk running across the half-dug foundations, sprinting through the factory, darting through the gates, sneaking into the rehearsal room, finding Smith and persuading her to accompany him back again.

Slowly, Tim's optimism faded. Time passed. Nothing happened. No one came. No noise broke the stillness. With each minute that passed, Tim felt more and more depressed.

Eventually, he decided that Grk was never coming back. The guards must have caught him.

Tim put his head in his hands. He felt exhausted and tearful. All his energy had disappeared. Things looked hopeless. Absolutely hopeless. This is it, thought Tim. This is the end.

He had done everything that he could possibly do, but he had failed. Bock would be here soon. He would shoot Tim and dump his body in the East River. No one would ever know what had happened.

Tim leaned against the wall opposite the door and waited for his executioner to arrive.

Chapter 27

The director was the last to leave the rehearsal room. He picked up his black bag, switched off the light and closed the door, then glanced at his watch. It was almost eleven o'clock at night. They had been rehearsing non-stop for the entire day. He shook his head and sighed.

'Long day, huh?'

The director jumped. He hadn't realised that anyone else was still in the building. He turned round and discovered one of the actresses standing beside him. She was the small, pretty girl with green eyes. The one with the odd name.

'Hello, Smith,' said the director. 'You did well today.'

'Really?'

The director nodded. 'You were very good. You're going to be okay.'

'Thanks,' said Smith. She pulled out her copy of the script. 'Actually, I did want to ask you about this one line.'

'Please, not now,' said the director. 'I've been here since nine o'clock this morning. Now I'm going to go home and go to bed. Then I'm going to get up, have a cup of coffee, take a shower and come back again. Let's talk about it tomorrow, okay?'

'Sure,' said Smith. She stuffed the script into her bag. 'Sorry.'

'No need to apologise,' said the director. He locked the

door of the rehearsal room. Together, they walked down the hallway to the exit. Smith opened the door. A few other actors were milling around in the street, saying good night to one another, heading in separate directions.

The director said to Smith, 'I have my car here. Do you want a lift? Which way are you going?'

'To the subway,' said Smith. 'And then Park Slope.'

'I'll drop you off. It's on my way.'

'Really? Thank you.' Smith smiled. She had never been quite sure if the director liked her. She hadn't been his first choice. He had originally given the part to another actress, who dropped out when she was offered a role in a movie. Throughout the rehearsal period, Smith had sensed that the director didn't really like her. More than anything, he seemed to ignore her.

Perhaps this was her big chance. If he gave her a lift home, she could chat to him. She could charm him with her wit and exuberance. Maybe he'd start to like her. When this play had finished, he might even offer her a part in another.

The director closed the door of the rehearsal rooms. The lock clicked shut. 'My car is this way,' he said, pointing down the street.

'Great.' Smith waved goodbye to the other actors. Together, Smith and the director strolled towards the car. The director said, 'So, are you enjoying the rehearsals?'

'Oh, yes,' said Smith. 'It's been a wonderful experience.'

'Excellent,' said the director. 'What have you enjoyed most?'

146

Smith thought carefully before answering. She knew it was important to say exactly the right thing. She opened her mouth – and saw a small white dog, running towards her as fast as his little legs would carry him.

Before the dog reached them, the director jumped backwards, throwing his arms in the air. 'Oh, my gosh,' he shouted. 'A dog! I hate dogs!' His black bag fell to the ground and smashed open, spilling papers and pencils. The director didn't care. He didn't even seem to notice. He just glared at the dog with angry eyes. 'Go away!' he hissed. 'Leave us alone!' But the dog didn't move or even glance at him. It was interested in some-one else. The dog stared at Smith.

Smith stared at the dog.

The director reached down and grabbed a pencil from the tarmac. He held it in his fist like a knife. He pointed the sharpened end at the dog. 'Don't come any closer,' he said. 'Just stay there.'

Smith looked at the small, white dog. Then she looked at the red-faced director clutching a pencil in his fist. She said, 'He's not going to bite you.'

'You don't know that,' said the director, retreating further behind Smith, making sure that she was between him and the dog. 'There are a lot of mad dogs in this city.'

'This dog isn't mad,' said Smith. She knelt down and stroked the dog's head. 'Hello, doggy,' she whispered. 'I know you, don't I?'

The dog nuzzled her hand with his wet nose.

Smith said, 'What's your name again? I've forgotten.'

The dog didn't answer.

There was a collar tied around his neck. Smith found a small metal tag attached to the collar. A few words and a telephone number were printed on the tag. 'That's right,' she whispered. 'You're Grk, aren't you?'

When Smith said his name, Grk barked twice. He darted backwards, turning his head excitedly from side to side. He looked at Smith, then he looked at the gates of Doctor Wiener's factory, then he looked at Smith again.

'He's going to bite,' shouted the director. 'He's mad! He's rabid! He's preparing to attack!' He jabbed the pencil in the dog's direction. 'Get back! Get away from me!'

Ignoring the director, Smith stared at the dog. She had the strange sense that he was trying to communicate something. But what? She whispered, 'What is it? What do you want?'

Grk barked again. He ran towards the gates, then ran back again to Smith, and barked once more. He lifted his head and looked at her with imploring eyes.

Smith said, 'Where's that boy? Tim – that's his name, right? Where's Tim?'

When Smith said Tim's name, Grk got even more excited. He ran towards the gates and then back again, barking repeatedly in short bursts. He sprinted round Smith's legs, circling her, then made another dash towards the gates of the factory.

'That's it,' said the director. 'I'm calling the police.' He knelt on the ground and scuffled through the contents of his bag, searching for his phone. He thrust aside pages from the script, a bottle of water, his diary, his iPod, two books and several more pencils until, right at the bottom of the bag, he finally found his phone. He pulled it out. To his relief, he saw that the phone was undamaged. He dialled 911, put the phone to his ear and looked up to see what had happened to Smith.

She had disappeared. And so had the dog.

The security guard opened the gate for Smith, but refused to let her into the yard. 'I'm sorry,' he said. 'Things have changed. No visitors allowed.'

Smith stared at him. She smiled with the same dazzling smile which had never previously failed to charm these guards. 'Oh, please,' she said. 'I've been rehearsing all day. All I want is one little hot dog.'

'Sorry, honey,' said the guard. 'I can't let you inside. We've had special orders.'

Grk waited at Smith's feet. He knew that he should keep quiet. He squatted on the ground, hidden from the guard's view.

Smith peered through the window. Inside the hut, the security guard was alone. He was watching *Seinfeld* on TV. Smith pointed at the screen. 'I love this episode.'

'Yeah, it's funny.'

'He's always funny.' Smith smiled. 'My cousin knows his sister.'

'Really?'

'Sure,' said Smith. She was lying, of course. But she was an actor, so she was good at lying. She said, 'He's going to come and see our play. The week after next.'

The guard's eyes widened with excitement. 'Really? Jerry Seinfeld will be at your play?'

'Sure,' said Smith. 'We're going to go out for dinner afterwards.' She stopped suddenly, as if an unexpected thought had just flashed across her mind. 'I tell you what,' she said. 'Why don't I get you tickets for the same night. You could come out to dinner with us. Meet Jerry.'

The guard blinked. A smile slowly spread across his face. 'I could come to dinner with Jerry Seinfeld?'

'You'd be very welcome to join us,' said Smith.

'Oh, my gosh,' said the guard. 'I would love that. I would really love that.'

'It's a done deal,' said Smith. She smiled, then sighed. 'You know, we're been rehearsing since nine o'clock this morning. I'm just exhausted. And so hungry.'

The guard glanced around the hut as if he was worried that someone might overhear him. Then he peered into the yard to check that they weren't being observed. Finally, he whispered to Smith, 'I wish I could let you inside. But the rules have changed today. No strangers. No intruders. We've had strict instructions.'

Smith fluttered her eyelashes at him. 'Not even little me?'

'I'm sorry,' said the guard. 'Not even you.'

'But I'll only be five minutes,' said Smith. 'I'll just grab a hot dog and run straight back. What possible harm could that do?'

The guard looked at her. There was something irresistible about her smile. There was also something irresistible about the thought of going to dinner with Jerry Seinfeld. And the guard knew that if he didn't let her inside to buy a hot dog, she wouldn't have any reason to take him to a restaurant with Jerry Seinfeld. The guard nodded. 'Go on,' he said. 'But be quick.'

Smith grinned. She promised to be back in two minutes. She blew a kiss to the guard and hurried across the yard towards the factory.

The guard sat down and settled in his chair. He stared at the TV screen. Jerry was joking with George and Elaine. Kramer was in the background, moving his body in that crazy way like he always did. The guard smiled. This time next week, he and Jerry would be sitting in a restaurant together. They'd have a few beers. They'd talk about the football. He would tell a few jokes, and maybe Jerry would laugh at them. Think of that. Jerry Seinfeld laughing at his jokes.

The guard was so involved in his daydream that he didn't notice Smith switching direction and heading towards a different part of the factory. Nor did he notice the small dog that was running ahead of her.

Smith and Grk sprinted through the factory. They ducked under an archway and ran through another, smaller yard. Smith had no idea where she was going. She just followed Grk.

Grk darted across one yard, then another, and finally disappeared around a corner. Smith sprinted to catch him. She found him on the other side, waiting for her. As soon as he saw her, he started running again.

They took a long, indirect route. Grk couldn't open any doors, so he had been unable to travel down any of the long corridors which cut through the heart of the factory. Instead, he had discovered a roundabout trail that ducked through dark yards, wriggled along a dusty alleyway, ran round the dustbins, crossed some newly-dug drains, circled a crane and a truck and a digger, and finally ended beside a big, old building with very dirty windows.

Each of the windows had thick metal bars over the glass. There were no lights. It was cold and gloomy.

As Smith drew closer, she could see that one of the windows had a pane punched out. That was the window that Grk headed towards.

Smith followed Grk across the uneven earth. Broken glass crunched under her feet. She reached the window and looked inside.

A small white face peered back at her.

Chapter 28

Talking through the broken window, Smith and Tim quickly discussed what had happened and what they should do next. The problem was quite simple. Smith and Grk were outside. Tim was inside. Separating them, there was a solid brick wall and a window blocked by thick metal bars. The three of them – a young boy, a thin woman and a small dog – could not possibly break the bars, knock down the wall or dig a hole under the concrete floor.

'I know exactly what to do,' said Smith. 'I'll find a door into the building. Then I'll come and fetch you.'

'But the door of this room is locked,' said Tim. 'With a key and two bolts. You wouldn't be able to open it.'

'Okay, okay,' said Smith, rubbing her forehead with her hands. 'Let me think.' She glanced around, searching for inspiration. She glanced along the building, then stared at the window. She wrapped the fingers of her right hand around one of the bars and pulled. It didn't budge. 'I know what to do,' said Smith. She reached into her bag and pulled out a mobile phone. 'My cousin works as a plumber. I'll ring him. He'll have tools. He can cut through these bars.'

Tim said, 'How long will that take?'

'Not long,' said Smith. 'An hour. Maybe even less. He lives in Queens.'

Tim explained that they probably didn't have an hour to spare. Bock was coming back at midnight.

Smith looked at her watch. It was half past eleven. 'Then I'll ring the police,' she said. 'They'll get here in fifteen minutes.'

'No,' said Tim. 'They'll have to come in through the main gates. The guards will warn Doctor Wiener. He'll have time to move me before letting the police into the factory.'

'Then I don't know,' said Smith. 'I just don't know. What can we do?'

They stood in silence, thinking. Smith rubbed her forehead. Tim bit his fingernails. Grk lay on the ground, taking care to avoid the broken glass.

Around them, the building site was silent and threatening. In the murky gloom, the big vehicles looked like freaky animals. The crane was a dinosaur with a long neck, bending down to nuzzle the ground. The trucks were massive rhinoceroses, flexing their armoured shoulders. The digger was a huge squatting bird, a puffin or a parrot, burrowing its fat beak into the earth.

'I've got it!' Tim clapped his hands together. 'I know what we can do.'

'Tell me,' said Smith.

Quickly, Tim explained his idea. He grinned, delighted with his own cleverness. 'It'll work. I know it will.'

'I'm sorry,' said Smith, shaking her head. 'I can't do that.'

'Why not?'

'Because I can't drive.'

'What do you mean? You're a grown-up! You're an American! Why can't you drive?'

'I do have a licence,' said Smith. 'I passed my test. But I haven't driven a car for, like, five years. I'm a New Yorker. We use the subway.'

Tim sighed. He shook his head slowly from side to side. He couldn't believe what was happening. Grk had managed to sneak out of the factory, find this woman, bring her back – and now she was refusing to drive! He took a deep breath. 'This is what you have to do,' he said. 'You're an actor, aren't you?'

'Yes.'

'Have you ever been in an action movie?'

Smith shook her head. 'I auditioned for an action movie once. The script was about this comet hitting the Earth. But I didn't get the part. I wasn't energetic enough, they said. I wasn't enough of an action hero. They said I was too nervous. Me? Nervous? I couldn't believe it. They said I have problems with my—'

But before she could describe any more of her problems, Tim interrupted her. 'So, you'd like to star in an action movie?'

'Sure,' said Smith, shrugging her shoulders, slightly offended that he should have interrupted her just as she was about to reveal some of her most personal issues.

'Imagine you're in an action movie,' said Tim. 'You're the heroine. This is the final scene. You have to get inside that digger. You have to drive it at this wall. And free me from prison. Okay? Can you do that?'

'I don't know,' said Smith. 'It's not so much—'

155

Once again, Tim interrupted her. He hissed, 'Shh!'

Smith blinked, amazed by his rudeness, but kept quiet.

'Listen,' whispered Tim. 'What's that?'

They both listened. Yes, there it was again: the sound of footsteps. Someone was walking down the corridor. Bock had come back. He was early.

Tim whispered, 'You have to do it now.' Through the thick door, he could hear the footsteps getting louder. Bock was coming closer. Very slowly, Tim whispered through the window, 'You can do it, Smith. You can do it.'

Smith closed her eyes. She breathed deeply and concentrated on acting a role. She was trying to be someone else. Not herself. Not Smith. Not a nervous New Yorker who couldn't drive. When she opened her eyes again, she would be an energetic action heroine who knew how to drive trucks and wouldn't even flinch at the thought of knocking down a big brick wall.

She opened her eyes. 'I'm ready,' she said. Her voice sounded different. All her fear was gone. Now, she was strong and confident and ready for action. 'Let's go!' She turned round and ran across the uneven earth, heading for the nearest digger. Grk ran after her.

The footsteps in the corridor got louder, then stopped. Bock was standing outside the room. There was a rattling noise. Tim knew what that meant. Bock was searching through his pockets, locating his keys.

Tim ran to the other end of the room. He stood against the wall. The shadows would hide him for a second, but no longer. But maybe that extra second would make a difference.

He heard the sound of a bolt being drawn. Click-clunk. Then another bolt. Click-clunk. That was followed by the sound of a key being fitted into the lock.

And then he heard another sound. The roar of an engine.

'Quick,' whispered Tim. 'Please, be quick.'

The key turned in the lock. Tim could see the door. The handle was turning. He pressed his back against the wall.

The engine got louder. It was coming closer. He could hear other sounds too. Clattering and smashing and crunching. He didn't know what they meant. Maybe Smith couldn't steer the digger. Maybe she was crashing into the crane or the trucks, rolling over drains and pipes.

The door swung open. Bock came into the room. He peered into the gloom. He said, 'Kid? Where are you?'

Tim didn't reply.

'No point hiding,' said Bock. 'You've got nowhere to hide.'

Tim stayed exactly where he was. He could feel the cold bricks against his back. He could hear the digger rolling across the earth, its engine moaning and protesting.

Bock clicked a switch on the wall outside the room, putting the light on. Tim and Bock stared at one another. Bock was dressed in a black suit and a white shirt. In his right hand, he was holding a pistol. He smiled. 'Let's go, kid. Time to meet the fishes.'

'I'd rather stay here,' said Tim.

157

Bock laughed. 'Sure you would. But you don't have much choice.' He raised the pistol and pointed it at Tim's head. 'Come on. Quick. Let's move.'

Tim took a step towards him. Then another step.

'I said quick,' said Bock. 'We don't have all night.'

At that moment, there was a deafening crash. Splinters wriggled along the wall. Dust and plaster flew into the air. Bricks fell forwards. Bock turned around, then stumbled backwards in astonishment.

The wall groaned. The whole earth seemed to be shaking. The splinters turned into cracks, and the cracks turned into holes, and the wall divided in half, and a huge yellow digger roared into the room, churning up the floor with its massive black tyres.

Tim sprang to one side. The digger's bucket smashed past him, missing his head by a couple of inches, and rammed into the next wall, knocking out bricks, smashing plaster, sending an avalanche of dust into the air.

There was no sign of Bock. He had disappeared, swallowed up by the swirling dust and falling bricks.

Smith was sitting in the digger's cab, screaming at the top of her voice. 'Where's the brake?' she shouted. 'Which one is the brake?' She pressed button after button, and pulled lever after lever, but couldn't locate the brake. The wheels spun round at full speed, trying to get a grip on the concrete floor, pushing and pushing against the wall.

Tim leaped over the pile of rubble. 'Run!' he shouted, beckoning to Smith. 'RUN!'

She couldn't hear his voice over the noise of the

engine, but she understood what he meant. She jumped down from the cabin. Grk jumped after her and bounded across the bricks towards Tim. Together, the three of them ducked through the hole in the wall and ran across the building site.

Behind them, the digger continued ramming forwards without a driver, thumping through the first wall and heading for the second. The building crumpled around it. Glass and bricks smashed to the ground. Dust and plaster floated into the air. If the digger continued like this, it would punch a hole straight through the middle of the building, come out the other side and continue all the way to Coney Island.

Tim and Grk and Smith ran towards the nearest truck.

None of them looked back. None of them saw a white figure emerging through the hole and stumbling across the rubble.

It was Bock. He was completely coated in dust. His black suit had turned white. His hair was white, his face was white, his shoes were white. Even his pistol was white.

But a pistol's colour isn't important. What matters is the finger on the trigger. And Bock's finger was still steady.

Bock wiped the dust from his eyes and peered into the gloom. He saw a crane and a truck. Between them, he could spot three small figures. Running away from him. A woman and a boy and a dog.

Bock gritted his teeth. He wasn't going to be beaten by a woman and a boy and a dog. Imagine if people found out! He knew what they'd say. Frank Bock.

159

Burglar, assassin, tough guy. Made to look like an idiot by a little boy. Oh, no, thought Bock. That isn't going to happen. No one is going to say that about me.

He raised the pistol, gripped the handle with both hands and aimed at the nearest of the three running figures. The little boy. The kid who had caused all this trouble in the first place. Aiming at the boy's head, Bock pulled the trigger.

Chapter 29

The bullet parted Tim's hair like a comb. He felt it scrape across the top of his head. He ducked and turned round. On the other side of the building site, he could see the shadowy shape of Bock, one arm raised, pointing a gun at him.

Tim darted from side to side, hoping the darkness would hide him. He heard another bullet whistling through the air, but it didn't touch him.

He reached the truck. Smith was already clambering into the cab. Tim grabbed Grk, tucked him under his arm, and scrambled after Smith. With a loud CRACK, a bullet pinged off the metal. Tim hauled himself into the cab and dropped Grk on the floor.

CRACK! Another bullet crashed against the truck.

It was time to go.

Tim looked around the cab. Surrounding the steering wheel, there were levers and dials and switches and knobs – and he had no idea what any of them did.

Nor did Smith. She was sitting in the driver's seat, staring at the controls. She had managed to switch on the engine, but she couldn't bring herself to drive the truck. It was just too big and scary.

'Go,' shouted Tim. 'The guards will be here any minute!'

But Smith couldn't act any more. The movie had

become too real. In movies, the bullets don't hurt. When you're filming a movie, you get a coffee and a doughnut between each take. That's why movies are so much better than real life, thought Smith.

Tim shoved her aside. He sat down and grabbed the wheel. But he was too short. He couldn't reach the accelerator.

Another bullet cracked against the metal and ricocheted across the cab. Tim could feel the whooooosh as the bullet whistled through the air. He grabbed Smith's sleeve. 'Push the accelerator!' he shouted, pointing at the floor of the cabin. 'PUSH THE ACCELERATOR!'

Smith put her foot on the accelerator. She pressed down. The truck lumbered forward.

Bock stopped to reload. He pulled the empty magazine from his pistol, tossed it on the ground, and grabbed a replacement from his back pocket. He looked up. The truck had started moving. Slotting the magazine into his pistol, he took aim at the cabin and fired three shots in quick succession.

BAM! BAM! BAM! Three bullets cracked into the back of the truck.

Trying to concentrate on nothing except driving, Tim turned the steering wheel. He pointed the truck towards the fence. Smith squatted at his feet, pushing her foot down on the accelerator. Grk nestled beside her.

On the rough ground, the truck bounced up and down, dipping into a drain and skidding on the soft, freshly-dug earth. Tim fought with the steering wheel, frantically trying to keep control. It was stronger than him. The truck seemed to be making its own decisions, lunging this way and that way, swerving from side to side, then leaping forwards.

The fence was ten feet tall and constructed from thick wire. Along the top, there were sharp spikes to discourage intruders.

But the strong wire and the sharp spikes were no protection against a yellow truck. The fence bulged, then snapped. Wire crackled like popping corn. The truck skidded into the road and roared away.

In the middle of the fence, there was a truck-sized hole. Bock ran across the building site, charged through the hole and stood in the middle of the street. He raised his gun and fired. BAM! BAM! He kept firing until the magazine was empty. BAM! BAM! BAM! BAM! BAM! Every bullet hit its target but each one pinged harmlessly off the back of the truck, doing nothing worse than denting the metal and scratching the paint.

Tim had no idea where he was going. The streets all looked the same. So he just drove straight ahead, trying to put as much distance as possible between the truck and the factory.

Shouting to be heard above the engine's roar, Smith leaned across the cabin and yelled, 'How do you know how to drive a truck?'

'I don't,' said Tim.

As they turned a corner, the edge of the truck punched against the side of a building, knocking out a few bricks.

Tim grappled desperately with the steering wheel, trying to make the truck go straight ahead, but the huge vehicle seemed to have its own idea about their destination.

With a crunch, the truck ploughed into a lamppost. The post snapped in half. The lamp crashed down onto the pavement. The bulb flickered, then went dark.

Tim twisted the steering wheel. The truck swerved across the road and smashed into a row of parked cars, clipping their wing mirrors.

Tim twisted the wheel in the opposite direction. The truck swerved again, knocking over another lamppost and ploughing into the back of another parked car, sending it spinning round and round in the middle of the road.

If Bock was following them, there would be an easy trail for him to track – a path of chipped bricks, broken glass, smashed cars and horizontal lampposts.

Chapter 30

Every Sunday night, Bobby Copper purchased a bottle of bourbon from the local store. He bought a cheese roll, a packet of peanuts and a bottle of their cheapest bourbon. He walked through the streets until he found a nice-looking bench or a quiet doorway. He sat down. He ate the cheese roll and the peanuts, washing them down with the bourbon. Then he fell asleep.

Tonight, Bobby was sitting on a bench opposite an old warehouse. He knew this warehouse, and he liked it.

It was the old carpet warehouse. Forty years ago, back when he was a child, they used to store carpets here. The warehouse had recently been sold to some fancy developer who had hired a fancy architect to convert the warehouse into fancy apartments. A year from now, the yuppies would be moving in.

Bobby sighed. Things were changing. He didn't like change.

He ate the cheese roll and drank half the bourbon. He was looking at the bottle, trying to decide whether it was half full or half empty, when he heard several strange noises.

He could identify one of the noises. It was a truck's engine. But there were other noises too, and he couldn't identify any of them. Crashing and smashing. Banging and tinkling. Scratching and scraping. As if ten guys with baseball bats were running down the street, destroying whatever they could find.

At that moment, a big yellow truck skidded round the corner and roared down the street, heading straight for Bobby.

He was too surprised to move. He just sat there, holding his bottle of bourbon, staring at the truck as it came closer and closer.

Tim didn't know what to do. The truck was stronger than him. And it was heading straight for a man sitting on a bench.

Tim peered through the windscreen. The man had a grey beard and a bald head. He was holding a bottle.

'Move!' shouted Tim. 'Run!'

But the man didn't move. He just sat there, waiting for the truck to knock him down.

Using all his strength, Tim hauled the steering wheel to the left.

The tyres screeched. The truck shuddered and jerked and changed direction. Now it was heading straight towards a brick wall.

Tim yelled a warning to Smith, then braced himself against the steering wheel. Smith removed her foot from the accelerator and put her shoulder against the dashboard. Grk did nothing. He didn't really understand what was happening.

With a crash that sounded like the end of the world, the truck rammed into the brick wall. The noise could be heard a mile away. Bricks flew through the air and pieces of truck went everywhere.

Bobby couldn't believe his eyes. First a truck comes roaring down the street. Then it crashes into the old carpet factory. And finally who gets out? Some tough guys? A couple of teenage runaways? No – a slim woman, a little boy and a dog.

Bobby looked at the bottle. Wow, he thought. This bourbon is stronger than it looks. He took another long sip.

When he put the bottle down, the woman, the boy and the dog had vanished.

Bobby shook his head.

Maybe I dreamed the whole thing, he thought.

Half an hour later, when the police arrived, that's exactly what they said too. Bobby told them about the truck coming round the corner and crashing into the old carpet factory. He described the woman, the boy and the dog getting down from the cab. He explained how they had disappeared into thin air.

The police officers sniffed Bobby's breath and looked at his bottle of bourbon. Then one of the officers said, 'Gramps, I reckon you dreamed the whole thing.'

Chapter 31

Tim, Grk and Smith walked quickly towards the nearest subway. When they had been walking for about ten minutes, Smith spotted a taxi. She jumped into the street and waved frantically. The taxi stopped. Smith opened the back door. Grk sprang inside, followed by Tim. Smith sat beside them and slammed the door.

The driver said, 'Where to?'

Smith looked at Tim. 'Where are you staying? Where are your folks?'

Tim said, 'Can we go to your house?'

'I don't have a house,' said Smith. 'I have an apartment.'

'Can we go there?'

'I guess so,' said Smith. She told the driver her address.

As the taxi accelerated along the street, Tim turned round and looked through the back window. The street was empty. Nothing moved. Not a car, not a bike, not a person. No one was following them.

Suddenly, he remembered something. 'Oh, gosh,' he said.

Smith looked at him. 'What's wrong?'

'I haven't eaten since breakfast.' Tim put his hand on his stomach. It felt flat. He looked at Smith. 'In your house – sorry, in your apartment – do you have any food?'

*

They ate at one o'clock in the morning. As far as Tim could remember, it was the latest that he had ever had supper in his entire life.

Smith cooked spaghetti. She heated up some meatballs and tomato sauce from the fridge. It was delicious, but Tim was too tired to eat. He managed a few mouthfuls, then his eyelids started to droop. He put down his fork and rested his head on his hands.

'Come on,' said Smith. 'You're sleeping on the couch.' She helped him to get up from the table.

'I have to clean my teeth,' said Tim.

'Where's your toothbrush?'

'I don't have a toothbrush.'

'Then you don't have to clean your teeth.'

Smith led Tim to the couch. She had already laid out a blanket and a couple of pillows.

Smith returned to the kitchen to clear up. Tim took off his shoes and socks, lay down and pulled the blanket over himself. Five seconds later, he was asleep.

Smith sat down and finished her supper. As she was eating, she glanced at the floor. Grk was sitting at her feet, staring at her with an imploring expression.

Smith looked at him. She said, 'Are you hungry?'

Grk didn't answer. He just stared at Smith. His eyes were big and round and sad.

'I guess you are,' said Smith.

She put Tim's plate on the floor. Grk jumped forwards, his tail wagging, and buried his nose in the pile of spaghetti.

Smith said, 'Do you like my cooking?'

Grk didn't answer. He was too busy eating.

'I'll take that as a yes,' said Smith. She picked up her fork. Together, Smith and Grk made their way through what remained of the spaghetti and the meatballs.

Chapter 32

Tim was woken by the sound of someone saying his name.

He sat up, blinking and rubbing his eyes. Bright sun-

Tim was woken by the sound of someone saying his name.

He sat up, blinking and rubbing his eyes. Bright sunlight was shining through the gaps between the curtains. For a moment, Tim couldn't understand where he was. Then he looked at the blanket and the couch, and remembered everything.

He could hear the noise of the television in the next room. He rolled off the couch and wandered into the kitchen.

Smith was sitting at the kitchen table, sipping tea and staring at the TV screen. A newsreader was reporting the disappearance of a British tourist. 'The NYPD is currently searching locations around Central Park,' said the newsreader. 'If you see this boy, please contact your local police department.' The screen was filled with a photograph of a face.

Tim recognised the face. It belonged to him.

The photograph was replaced by the newsreader, who went on to the next story. A whale had been washed ashore in the Hamptons.

Grk wandered round the kitchen table, wagging his tail. He came to say hello to Tim, who squatted on the floor and tickled Grk's ears.

'You'd better ring your parents,' said Smith. 'I think they're pretty worried about you.'

'They'll be fine,' said Tim. 'They're always fussing about something.'

But Smith insisted, threatening that she wouldn't give Tim any breakfast if he didn't ring his parents. She looked up the number of the Millard Fillmore Inn and handed the phone to Tim. He dialled. A receptionist answered. Tim asked to be put through to the Malts. When he heard his mother's voice, Tim said, 'Hi, Mum. It's me.'

'Oh, my God.' His mother sounded distraught. 'Where are you? What's happening? Where have you been?'

'I'm fine,' said Tim.

'But where are you?'

'In New York.'

'Tim,' said his mother. 'Tell me exactly where you are.'

'I'll be back tonight,' said Tim. 'I'll meet you at the hotel. Okay?'

'No, that is not okay.' Now his mother sounded cross. 'You are not coming here tonight. You are coming back here right now this minute.'

'Mum, please,' said Tim. 'Don't treat me like a child.'

'But you are a child!'

'Maybe I am,' said Tim. 'But that doesn't mean you have to treat me like one.'

'Now listen to me, Timothy Malt. Tell me exactly where you are.'

'I can't.'

'Why not?'

'I don't know where I am.'

'Oh, Timothy. What's going on? Where have you been? Who are you with?'

'I'll see you tonight,' said Tim. 'Bye.'

'Wait. Timothy? Timothy!'

Tim took the phone away from his ear. He could hear his mother's voice squeaking at him through the receiver. He switched the phone off and handed it to Smith. 'Thanks,' he said. 'Did you say something about breakfast?'

They went to a café on the same block as Smith's apartment. They sat outside so Grk could sit with them. Smith had coffee and a blueberry muffin. Tim had freshly-squeezed orange juice and waffles with maple syrup. Grk had whatever Tim and Smith couldn't eat.

Smith spent some time trying to persuade Tim to return to his parents. But Tim refused. 'I have a job to do,' said Tim. 'I have to retrieve the Golden Dachshund. I know where it is. I just have to go and get it.'

Smith said, 'But won't Doctor Wiener be hiding the Golden Dachshund right now?'

'He certainly will,' said Tim. 'That's why we have to get moving as quickly as possible.'

'But what are we going to do?'

Tim smiled. 'I have an idea.'

'It'd better be a good one.'

'I think it is. And it might even work. But only if you help.'

'Me?' Smith glanced at her watch. 'I have to be at my rehearsals in an hour and ten minutes. How long will it take?'

'The whole day,' said Tim. 'You'll have to ring and say you're sick.'

173

'I can't do that. Our first night is next week.'

Tim leaned forward. 'You have to make a choice, Smith. Which is more important? Your rehearsals or saving the Golden Dachshund?'

'My rehearsals,' said Smith. 'No contest. I don't know anything about the Golden Dachshund.'

Tim sighed. 'But without you, I can't do it. Please, Smith. I need your help.'

Smith didn't know what to say. The play started next week. If she missed a day of rehearsals, perhaps the director would find a replacement to do her part. New York was full of actors. Anyway, she hardly knew Tim. And she knew absolutely nothing about this dachshund. She shook her head. 'I'm sorry, Tim, but I have to go to my rehearsal.'

Tim said, 'There'll be a reward.'

'I don't care about money,' said Smith. 'I'm an artist. I only care about my craft.'

'But that's the whole point about my plan,' said Tim. 'You have to act. In fact, you'll have to act better than you've ever acted in your entire life.'

Smith was intrigued. 'That's sounds interesting,' she said. 'Tell me more.'

'Will you help?'

'When I've heard your plan, I'll decide.'

Tim glanced at the other tables in the café. He didn't like revealing his brilliant plan in public. What if someone was eavesdropping? What if one of the other people in the café was a criminal or a journalist or a friend of Doctor Wiener's? Or all three?

174

But Tim finally decided that he didn't have any choice. In a low whisper, he explained his plan.

By the time that Tim finished his explanation, Smith had a huge grin on her face. She shook her head slowly from side to side. 'You know what, Tim? You are a genius.'

'Thanks,' said Tim. 'Does that mean you'll help?'

'I guess it does.'

'Great,' said Tim. 'Can I use your phone?'

Smith reached into her bag and pulled out her phone. She passed it across the table.

Tim took a white card from his pocket. There was a name and a number printed on the card. Tim dialled the number. 'Hello,' said Tim. 'Is that Andy Kielbasinski?'

Chapter 33

At three o'clock in the afternoon, a yellow taxi stopped outside the front gate of Doctor Wiener's factory in Brooklyn. The taxi's back door opened and three figures stepped out: a woman, a dwarf and a dog.

The woman was thin and very beautiful. She had long black hair and bright red lips. She was wearing a green dress. If you were a connoisseur of fashion, you would have recognised that her bag had been designed by Miuccia Prada and her shoes had been made by Manolo Blahnik.

The dwarf had long hair, a thick moustache and a beard which covered much of his face. He was wearing a black suit, black socks and black shoes.

The dog was a poodle with a shaggy black coat.

If you knew a great deal about dogs, you might have said that this particular poodle looked a little unusual. In fact, he didn't look much like a poodle at all. He was too small. His ears were the wrong shape. His coat was suspiciously similar to an old wig.

But if you didn't know much about dogs, you would just have thought, 'Oh, look at that sweet little poodle.'

Before the woman, the dwarf and the poodle could go anywhere, the driver jumped out of his taxi and shouted after them, 'Hey, lady! You haven't paid me!'

'I am most extremely sorry,' said the woman in a strong German accent. She pulled a gold purse from her Prada handbag and removed a hundred dollar bill. 'Please to keep the change,' she said, handing the bill to the driver.

The driver blinked. He hadn't been tipped so much in all his twenty-three years of driving a taxi. 'Thank you,' he stuttered. 'Thank you very much.'

'It is my pleasure,' said the woman. Her German accent was so strong that it was almost incomprehensible. 'Could you tell me, please, how should we be entering this factory?'

'I'll ring the doorbell for you,' said the driver. He hurried to the gate. 'Open up,' he shouted into the intercom. 'You got visitors.'

The gate slowly eased open. Two security guards peered curiously at the taxi driver, his passengers and their dog.

'Thank you so much,' said the woman to the taxi driver. 'And is there any possibility that you might wait for us? We will be, perhaps, one half of one hour.'

'I'll be right here,' said the driver. 'Take as long as you like.' For the chance of another tip like that, he would be happy to wait all day.

The driver returned to his taxi. The woman walked through the gate, followed by the dwarf and the poodle.

'Good afternoon,' said one of the security guards. On their security cameras, the guards had seen the woman paying the taxi driver with a hundred dollar bill and not asking for any change. They knew that she must be rich or influential, and probably both. So they were extremely polite. The second security guard smiled and said, 'Can we help?'

In her strong German accent, the woman said, 'We have come to pay a visit to Doctor Wiener.'

'Very good, ma'am,' said the guard. 'Please, come inside. I'll tell him you're here.'

Chapter 34

The woman, the dwarf and the poodle walked slowly across the yard, accompanied by one of the security guards. He led them through a corridor, across another yard and into a shabby office block. Ruby was sitting behind her desk. She smiled at the visitors and told the guard to take them upstairs.

Doctor Wiener was waiting for them in his office. Frank Bock stood by the door, guarding the exit and watching for any sudden movements.

Doctor Wiener dismissed the security guard and peered curiously at his guests. He had the odd sense that he had seen them somewhere before. But he couldn't remember where or when. He said, 'Have we met before?'

'I think not,' said the woman in her strong German accent.

Doctor Wiener stared suspiciously at the woman, the dog and the dwarf. Something about the dwarf niggled at his memory. He looked at the woman and said, 'Are you sure?'

'I am sure,' said the woman. 'We have never met before.'

'You certainly look familiar.'

'Perhaps you have seen my photograph in a magazine. Do you read *Paris Match*, perhaps? Or *OK*? Or *Hello!*?'

'You're famous?'

'That is correct,' said the woman. 'Please, let me introduce myself. My name is Countess Sonja von Dachswagen.'

'Never heard of you, honey,' said Doctor Wiener. 'What are you, German?'

'I am Austrian.' She patted the dwarf on his head. 'This is Hans. My dwarf.'

'*Guten Morgen*,' said Hans.

As you probably know, '*Guten Morgen*' actually means 'Good morning' in German, which is a pretty strange thing to say at three o'clock in the afternoon. But Doctor Wiener didn't seem to mind. He just blinked at Hans, then glared at the Countess. 'He's your dwarf?'

'*Ja, ja*,' said Countess Sonja von Dachswagen. 'In Austria, all the best families have their own dwarves.'

'Oh, really.' Doctor Wiener nodded. 'I didn't know that.' He pointed at Grk. 'And what's that? A poodle?'

'*Ja*, this is a poodle. My other twelve dogs are dachshunds.'

'You have twelve dachshunds?'

'*Ja, ja*. But they do not like to travel. Only the poodle will eat the foreign food. So the dachshunds stay home with my husband in the Schloss Dachswagen. Perhaps you have heard of our schloss?'

Doctor Wiener shook his head. 'A schloss? What's a schloss? Is that like dental floss?'

'*Nein, nein*.' The Countess chortled. 'A schloss is a castle.'

180

'And you want to sell it? No, thanks. Not interested. I'm happy living here.'

'*Nein, nein,*' said the Countess with a patient smile. 'I am not interested in selling my schloss or anything else. I have an invitation for you. Next month, the Royal Association of European Dachshunds will be holding our annual show in the Schloss Dachswagen, and we would like to invite the famous Doctor Wiener. We wish you to be our guest of honour.'

'Me.' Doctor Wiener looked as if he wasn't sure whether to laugh or cry. 'You want me to be your guest of honour?'

'That is correct,' said the Countess. 'We wish to honour your services to dachshunds. Your art collection is famous all over the world.'

Doctor Wiener looked nervous. 'My art collection? What do you know about my art collection?'

'Very little,' said the Countess. 'Only rumours. But I have heard...' She lowered her voice to a whisper. 'I have heard rumours that your art collection is most magnificent.'

'Well, now.' Doctor Wiener blushed. 'It's not bad.'

'*Wunderbar,*' sighed the Countess. Leaning forward, she fluttered her eyelashes and smiled beautifully, showing her perfect teeth. 'Might it be possible to see this magnificent collection of dachshund art?'

Doctor Wiener glanced at Bock. 'I don't know,' said Doctor Wiener. 'We've been having a little trouble. In fact, the collection is moving today. Going to a new location.'

The Countess nodded. 'Where are you taking it?'

'I can't tell you.' Doctor Wiener shrugged his shoulders. 'For security reasons. I'm sure you understand.'

'Of course I understand,' sighed the Countess. 'Security is most important. But we have travelled all the way from Vienna to see this collection. Could we not sneak one little peek?'

Doctor Wiener looked at her. He was worried, but he was also quite excited. It wasn't every day that a Countess came to his factory and flattered his taste in art. Excusing himself, Doctor Wiener walked to the other end of the room and held a whispered conference with Bock. They talked for about five minutes, discussing different options, and then Doctor Wiener returned. He had a beaming smile on his face. 'Just for you, Countess,' he said. 'I'm going to open the collection and give you a private tour.'

'*Wunderbar!*' The Countess clapped her hands together. 'Oh, thank you, thank you. The Archduke of Bavaria is going to be so jealous. The Queen of Sweden will never forgive me for coming here without her. You know they are all great lovers of dachshunds – and they have all wished to see the famous art collection of the *wunderbar* Doctor Wiener.'

'Fabulous,' stammered Doctor Wiener. He was blushing. His cheeks had gone bright pink with pleasure. 'That's fabulous.' He felt almost faint with excitement at the thought of all those European monarchs discussing his art collection. 'Please, your Royal Highness, follow me.' He hauled his bulk across the room to the huge map

182

of New York and pressed a red dot with his pudgy forefinger. The map slid sideways along the wall, revealing a dark passageway.

'How exciting,' said the Countess. 'This is for the security, *ja*?'

'That is correct,' said Doctor Wiener. 'This is the secret entrance to my art collection. Please, follow me.' He waddled down the passageway. The Countess walked after him, followed by the dwarf and the poodle. Bock came last.

Bock pressed a hidden button. Behind him, the map slid shut.

Chapter 35

They walked down the dark passageway. After about fifty paces, they reached a fork and turned right. The passageway continued for another fifty paces, then came to a door. Doctor Wiener reached under his shirt. Hanging on a gold chain around his neck, he had a key. He turned the key in the lock and opened the door.

'Welcome to my museum,' said Doctor Wiener.

He led them through the door and into a long windowless room. The walls were grey. Pale lights were embedded in the low ceiling. The air felt cool and fresh.

Countess von Dachswagen walked into the middle of the room, followed by her dwarf and her poodle.

The poodle lifted his nose into the air and sniffed several times, hoping he might be able to detect a frankfurter or a nice white bun or even a few crumbs left over from someone else's lunch.

The Countess looked up and down the room, and shook her head in astonishment. '*Wunderbar*,' she whispered. 'This is utterly *wunderbar*.'

Her dwarf stood beside her. He looked up and down the room too. He was searching for something. But he couldn't see it.

In the room, there were six sculptures and fifteen paintings. Every one of them depicted a dachshund.

If an art historian had walked into the room, he would have shaken his head in astonishment – and then rung the police. Half the artworks in the room had been bought for vast sums in auction houses. The other half had been stolen from museums in Europe and America.

Hanging at the far end of the room, there was Pablo Picasso's painting, *Le Chien Chaud*, which had not been seen in public for sixty years. It had disappeared during the Second World War, and had never been found.

Standing in the middle of the room, there was a long, skinny sculpture by Giacometti called *Signor Cane Caldo*. In 2002, it had been sold at Sotheby's in London for four million pounds. The buyer's identity had never been revealed.

There was a little portrait of a dachshund painted by Hans Holbein in 1535. There was a big photograph of three dachshunds standing on a pebbly beach which Bill Brandt had taken in 1967. There was a wooden carving of a dachshund by Alexander Calder and a marble sculpture of a dachshund by Auguste Rodin and a tiny sketch by Leonardo da Vinci, showing a small dog with a long body and very short legs.

When Doctor Wiener saw the Countess staring at the da Vinci sketch, he smiled. 'That's my favourite,' he said. 'Oh, it cost me a lot. But it was worth every cent. You know, I have made a fortune from frankfurters, but I've spent just about all of it on buying art. Or paying someone to steal it. Heh-heh-heh-heh.'

185

The Countess laughed with him. 'Oh, you are such a clever man,' she said. 'You know what you want and you get it. Am I right?'

'You are right,' said Doctor Wiener. 'You are exactly right. I know what I want and I get it. Heh-heh-heh-heh.'

The Countess leaned forward. In a low voice, as if she was telling a great secret, she whispered, 'And this man here...' She gestured at Bock, who was standing beside the door, guarding the entrance. 'Does he do some stealing?'

Doctor Wiener nodded. 'Bock is one of the greatest thieves that the world has ever seen. But let me assure you, he is also extremely well paid. In a year, he never earns less than one million dollars.'

'*Wunderbar*,' whispered the Countess. She glanced at her dwarf and her poodle. Then she looked back at Doctor Wiener. 'There is one other thing,' she said. She gestured at the paintings and sculptures in the museum. 'This is *wunderbar*. Utterly *wunderbar*. But I had hoped to see one particular sculpture.'

Doctor Wiener smiled. 'And what sculpture is that?'

'The Golden Dachshund,' said the Countess.

Doctor Wiener blinked. His mouth opened. He turned to look at Bock, as if seeking some kind of support, then he turned back again to look at the Countess. 'I don't know nothing about no Golden Dachshund,' he said.

The Countess smiled. She had a dazzling smile. 'Oh, come on, Doctor Wiener,' she said. 'This is not true. You have the Golden Dachshund. I know you do.'

Doctor Wiener's eyes were cold and hard. He said, 'How do you know?'

'It is simple,' replied the Countess. 'No one else would be clever enough to steal it.'

'Flattery will get you nowhere,'said Doctor Wiener. But a big smile spread across his face and a scarlet blush spread across his cheeks. There was something about the Countess's dazzling smile which he found irresistible. In the hot dog business, Doctor Wiener didn't get to spend much time with beautiful women. Particularly beautiful women with aristocratic connections who had travelled all the way from Vienna just to see him and his art collection. 'Wait a second,' he said. 'I have to talk to Bock.'

Doctor Wiener waddled across the room and had an earnest conversation with Bock. Left to themselves, the Countess and her dwarf started inspecting the paintings on the wall, trying to look as if they couldn't care less what Doctor Wiener was discussing with Bock.

The discussion ended when Doctor Wiener issued an order. Bock nodded. He walked to the other end of the museum and opened a hidden doorway which led to a storeroom. He was gone for less than a minute. When he returned, he was carrying the Golden Dachshund. He brought it to the centre of the room and placed it carefully on the floor.

The Countess, her dwarf and her poodle stared at the Golden Dachshund.

'There it is,' said Doctor Wiener. 'The Golden Dachshund.'

'Oh, my goodness,' whispered the Countess. 'It is beautiful.' She turned to look at her dwarf. 'It is most beautiful, *ja*?'

The dwarf nodded.

'Your dwarf doesn't speak much,' said Doctor Wiener.

'He is a dwarf of few words,' said the Countess. 'Now, you must tell me one thing. How did you get your hands on this Golden Dachshund?'

Doctor Wiener shook his head. 'Please, Countess, don't ask me questions like that. Some things are better kept secret.'

'I understand,' said the Countess. 'But this is truthfully the Golden Dachshund?'

'Oh, yes.' Doctor Wiener leaned down and stroked the dachshund's head as if it was a real dog. 'This is the real thing. The one and only Golden Dachshund. A week ago, this was locked in a bank vault. And now it belongs to me. Heh-heh-heh-heh.'

At that moment, a phone started ringing.

'Excuse me,' said the Countess. 'That must be my telephone.' She reached into her Prada handbag and withdrew a phone. She answered it. 'Hello? Yes. Yes. Of course.' She handed the phone to Doctor Wiener. 'It is for you.'

Doctor Wiener was very surprised. 'For me?'

'Yes, for you.'

Doctor Wiener stared at the phone for a minute. He

wasn't sure whether he should take it from the Countess. He stared at her, then at Bock. Neither of them said a word. Eventually, Doctor Wiener decided that a phone couldn't do him any harm. He took it and said, 'Hello?'

'Hello, Doctor Wiener,' said the voice on the other of the phone. 'This is the New York Police Department.'

Outside the factory, the taxi driver was still waiting for his passengers, hoping for another big tip.

Another car was now parked alongside the taxi. Inside, Andy Kielbasinski was sitting in the driver's seat, talking into a phone. He said, 'My name is Andy Kielbasinski. I'm waiting at the gates of your factory. I would be grateful if you'd come and meet me here.'

'I'm busy right now,' said Doctor Wiener.

'You're soon going to be a lot busier.'

'What's that supposed to mean?'

'I have your confession on tape,' said Andy Kielbasinski. 'I think you'd better come down to the precinct and discuss it with me.'

Back in the museum, Doctor Wiener was getting angry. His face was bright red. His fingers were clenched tightly round the phone. He said, 'My confession? What confession? What are you talking about?'

'For the last thirty minutes, I have recorded every word that you have said,' replied Andy Kielbasinski. 'You might as well come quietly, Doctor Wiener. You've told the New York Police Department exactly what we need to know about the theft of the Golden Dachshund.'

Doctor Wiener's face went bright red. He looked at the Countess. Suddenly, everything was beginning to make sense.

The Countess smiled back at him.

Doctor Wiener's eyes turned dark with fury. He dropped the phone on the ground. For a second, they could hear Andy Kielbasinski's voice squeaking. Then Doctor Wiener put his foot on the phone and pressed down with all his weight, crushing the phone into a flat pile of shattered plastic.

When the connection went dead, Andy Kielbasinski immediately called his headquarters and asked for reinforcements.

He had come to the factory alone. This was his big chance. If he did this right – if he helped to retrieve the Golden Dachshund and put Doctor Wiener behind bars – he would definitely get a promotion. He wouldn't have to spend his days in Central Park, helping tourists and picking up garbage. He would be given some proper police work to do.

Andy jumped out of the car. He hurried towards the gate and shouted at the guards, ordering them to let him inside.

The museum was silent. Doctor Wiener looked at the Countess. 'Who are you?' he said. 'What is this all about?'

'My name is Countess Sonja von Dachswagen.'

'No, it's not,' said Doctor Wiener. 'That was a good story and you had me fooled. But now it's time to tell the truth. Who are you?'

Before the Countess could respond, her dwarf stepped forward. The dwarf reached up to his face and grabbed his beard with both hands. He pulled it. The beard and moustache came loose. The dwarf threw the beard on the floor and pulled off his wig.

Doctor Wiener stared at him in amazement. 'You!'

'Yes,' said Tim. 'It's me.' With a smile, Tim unbuttoned the top two buttons of his shirt, reached inside, and pulled out a black wire. There was a small black blob attached to the end of the wire. Tim held the blob towards Doctor Wiener. 'Do you have anything else you'd like to say?'

Doctor Wiener stared at the blob. 'What is that?'

'A microphone,' replied Tim. 'We've recorded every word that you've been saying. The police are outside. You might as well come quietly.'

'Sure,' said Doctor Wiener. 'Whatever you say. I'll come quietly.'

He smiled.

And then, with surprising speed for such a fat man, he reached down, grabbed the Golden Dachshund from the floor, and ran towards the door.

Tim whistled at the poodle.

The poodle knew exactly what to do. He jumped forwards, opened his mouth and buried his sharp white teeth in Doctor Wiener's ankle.

Doctor Wiener screamed and stumbled.

Tim threw himself across the room and wrapped his arms around Doctor Wiener's other ankle.

A thinner, fitter, better-balanced man would have been able to shake them off. But Doctor Wiener was top-heavy. He was handicapped by his immense bulk. With a boy and a dog attached to both his ankles, he wasn't going anywhere. He yelled and wobbled and twisted and turned. Then he toppled towards the ground. With a THUD, he slammed into the concrete floor.

Just before he hit the floor, he threw the Golden Dachshund across the room. It soared through the air.

Bock caught it with both hands. He ducked through the doorway and sprinted down the passageway, holding the Golden Dachshund.

Tim and the poodle ran towards the door.

Over his shoulder, Tim shouted, 'Keep him here!'

And then he was gone, sprinting down the passageway in pursuit of Bock. The poodle galloped alongside him.

Countess Sonja von Dachswagen dropped her Prada handbag, kicked off her Manolo Blahnik shoes and removed her long black wig. You don't need me to tell you who emerged from the disguise. I'm sure you guessed several pages ago.

Smith walked barefoot across the room and stood above Doctor Wiener. He was unconscious. His eyes were shut. 'You stay like that,' said Smith. 'The police will be here in two minutes and I really don't want to

192

have to hit you.' But she picked up one of her shoes and held it above his head, poised to strike, just in case his eyes opened.

Chapter 36

If Tim had been thinking clearly, he would have stayed in the museum with Smith and the unconscious Doctor Wiener, waiting for the police to arrive. When Andy Kielbasinski charged through the door, Tim would have pointed in the direction which Bock had fled and let the police chase after him. Policemen were trained to tackle dangerous criminals. And they had guns.

But Tim wasn't thinking clearly. Having worked so hard to recapture the Golden Dachshund, he wasn't going to let someone run off with it. Particularly if that someone was a nasty piece of work like Frank Bock.

Tim sprinted down the passageway, pursued by the poodle. At the fork, they stopped and listened.

There! Tim could hear the distant rattle of footsteps. They were coming from the left-hand turning.

Tim started running in the direction of the footsteps. The poodle ran after him. After a few paces, the poodle's coat of curly black fur slipped off and fell to the floor. Without the weight of the wig, Grk ran even faster.

After fifty paces, Tim and Grk reached the end of the passageway and found themselves at a dead end. The passageway finished at a blank wall. There was no lock or handle.

Tim lifted his hand and ran his fingers along the wall.

The surface felt cold and smooth. The wall wasn't made of brick, stone or concrete. It was made of wood.

Tim remembered entering the passageway. The entrance had been covered by a map of New York. When Bock emerged from the passageway, he must have closed the sliding-door behind him.

Now, Tim was standing on the wrong side of the map.

Somewhere, there must be a switch or a lever. Of course, Bock would have known its whereabouts. If Tim could find the switch or the lever, he could press it or turn it, operating the mechanism to open the door. But he didn't have time to search for any switches or levers. With every second that passed, Bock was getting further away.

Tim looked down at Grk. He said, 'Wish me luck.'

Grk wagged his tail.

Tim curled his hand into a fist. He drew his arm back. As hard as he could, he rammed his fist into the centre of the blank wall.

Chapter 37

On the corner of Fifth Avenue and 21st Street, a couple of blocks from Madison Square, a hole appeared in New York City.

A hand came through the hole.

The first hand was followed by another hand.

Together, the two hands shredded holes in New York. They ripped out chunks of Manhattan and pulled down boroughs of Brooklyn. The two hands smashed a hole in the city that stretched from Hoboken to Coney Island.

When the hole was big enough, Tim thrust Grk through it, and jumped after him. They were back in Doctor Wiener's office. There was no sign of Bock. The door was open.

'Let's go,' said Tim. Together, he and Grk ran out of the door.

They didn't have time to wait for the lift, so they sprinted to the end of the corridor, charged through the double doors and jogged down the stairs, taking them two at a time.

On the ground floor, they barged through another set of double doors and found themselves in the reception area. Behind the desk, a blonde woman was slumped in her chair, reading a magazine.

Tim said, 'Hello, Ruby.'

The woman stared at him. 'It's you again,' she said.

'Now, you have to tell me. Where do I know you from?'

'A man just came through here,' said Tim. 'His name is Bock. Do you know him?'

'Of course I know Mr Bock,' said Ruby.

'Which way did he go?'

Usually, Ruby wouldn't have answered a question like that. She had earned her job as receptionist for Doctor Wiener by being exceptionally discreet. All kinds of strange things happened in this office, and Ruby never revealed any of them to anyone. But this kid knew her name. And she was sure that she knew him from somewhere. So she told him what he wanted to know. 'That way,' said Ruby, pointing at the door that led to the factory. 'But you gotta tell me. Where do I know you from?'

Tim didn't have time to answer. He turned and ran through the door, followed by Grk.

Ruby stared after him. She shook her head. Mrs Barton's nephew, the one who was so good at Scrabble, lived in Texas. This kid didn't have a Texan accent. He definitely wasn't the same kid that she met at Thanksgiving. So how did he know her name?

Tim and Grk sprinted down a long corridor, charged through two more doors and found themselves in the main room of the factory. He had been here yesterday. Nothing had changed since then. Meat and spices still swooshed through the tubes. Huge blades continued to stir the frothing cauldrons. An unending supply of frankfurters dropped onto a conveyer belt. Working this machinery, pulling levers and clicking switches and

197

checking dials and watching the sausages, there were about a hundred men and women, wearing white coats, white caps, white gloves and white masks.

Bock was walking briskly through the factory. He ducked under one of the large tubes and strode past the cauldrons. The workers glanced at the golden statue in his arms, but none of them stopped him. None of them even questioned his presence.

Tim stared across the room at Bock's retreating back.

What could Tim do? Bock was stronger and faster than him. And Bock was on the other side of the factory. In a moment, he would reach the door. Then he would escape to the yard. He probably had a car waiting. He would get away with the Golden Dachshund, melt it down, sell the gold and live comfortably for the rest of his life.

I can't let that happen, thought Tim. I have to do something. I have to stop him. But how?

Tim looked around. He stared at Grk.

Grk stared back.

'Think,' said Tim. 'Think!'

Grk just continued staring at him.

Tim looked up and down the long room. He ran his eyes along the cauldrons and the tubes and the hundreds of hot dogs popping out of the machinery, dropping onto the fast-moving conveyer belt. He looked at the workers. He stared at their faces, half-hidden by white masks, and their hands, protected by white gloves.

None of them could help him.

Or could they?

He turned round. Above the door through which he had entered the room, there was a red light. Beside the door, there was an intercom attached to the wall. And there was something else attached to the wall beside the intercom. A microphone.

Tim pressed the button, switching on the microphone. In an exceptionally gruff voice, he shouted into the receiver, 'Stop that man!'

His voice echoed round the factory, booming from every loudspeaker. 'STOP THAT MAN!'

A hundred white-coated workers looked up from their work. None of them realised that a small boy was shouting at them. Hearing the voice booming from the loudspeakers, they assumed that it belonged to the Chief of Security.

'STOP HIM!' shouted Tim. His voice boomed again, even louder. 'STOOOOP HIIIIIM!'

The workers stared at Bock. But none of them moved. None of them left their posts.

Bock walked briskly across the factory. He was twenty feet away from the door. He had twenty more paces to take. And when he had taken those twenty paces, he would be free.

'There is a reward of five hundred dollars,' shouted Tim into the microphone. His voice thundered through the loudspeakers. 'IF YOU STOP THAT MAN, EVERY SINGLE ONE OF YOU WILL RECEIVE FIVE HUNDRED DOLLARS!'

Bock was ten paces from the door. He knew what would happen next. He started running.

All around the factory, the workers dropped whatever they were doing and charged at Bock.

Bock reached the door. He grabbed the handle. He opened the door. Just as he was preparing to fling himself through the doorway and into the yard, a hand in a white glove grabbed the back of his jacket.

Bock tried to shake off the hand. But another gloved hand grabbed his other shoulder. The hands pulled him back into the factory. Bock stumbled. The door swung shut.

Dropping the Golden Dachshund, Bock thrust his hand under his jacket and reached for his gun. But he didn't have the time or the space to pull it out. More hands grabbed him from every angle. White gloves held his arms and his legs. A hundred workers surged forward, trying to get a piece of Bock.

'No,' shouted Bock. 'He's lying! No!'

But they ignored him. More and more hands arrived every second. Bodies pressed together. Slowly, Bock sank under the pressure of a hundred men and women in white coats. They pushed him to the floor.

Tim grinned. Bock wasn't going anywhere. Nor was the Golden Dachshund.

Chapter 38

Tim sat at the head of the long table. He had Smith on his right and Andy Kielbasinski on his left. For the past couple of minutes, none of them had said a word. They had been too busy eating.

Finally, Andy Kielbasinski dabbed his mouth with a napkin and broke the silence. 'This food is magnificent,' he said. 'Am I right?'

'You're right,' said Smith. 'It's fabulous. This is the best lobster bisque I've ever tasted. How about you, Tim? You like it?'

'Yes, it's very nice,' said Tim.

'Is this the best lobster bisque you've ever tasted?'

'Definitely,' said Tim.

He didn't admit that this was the first lobster bisque he had ever tasted. He wasn't even quite sure what a 'bisque' might be. But it certainly tasted very good.

They were sitting in a private dining room of the Four Seasons, one of the best restaurants in New York. There were twelve people sitting at the table, eating the finest food that the Four Seasons' kitchens could offer. Their host was Theodore W. Snag.

As a senior partner of Cumberland Fire & Theft Insurance Company, Theodore W. Snag had been responsible for insuring the contents of apartment 153, the Bramley Building, New York City. He had valued the Golden Dachshund at ten million dollars. Without the help of Tim and Grk, the Cumberland Fire & Theft Insurance Company would have been ten million dollars poorer.

To say thank you, Theodore W. Snag gave a thousand dollars to King Jovan's maid, repaying Tim's taxi fare twenty times over. He bought three new bikes and helmets for Dino, the bike-rental man in Central Park. He paid five hundred dollars to each of the workers who had prevented Bock escaping from the factory. Finally, he hired a private room at the Four Seasons and laid on the best lunch in New York.

King Jovan sat at one end of the table, with Max on his right and Natascha on his left. The Queen and her maid sat beside the Director of the National Museum and Theodore W. Snag. The Malts came next, then Smith and Andy Kielbasinski, either side of Tim.

And what about Grk? Where was he?

Dogs weren't allowed in the Four Seasons restaurant.

Actually, that's not quite true. Dogs weren't usually allowed in the restaurant. But since Theodore W. Snag had hired a private room, then paid a special 'dog tax', the management made an exception for one small black and white dog.

Grk stood on the floor beside Tim's chair. The waiters had brought a special plate for him. He was slowly making his way through a 14 oz steak, cooked medium rare, with french fries on the side.

When Grk finished the steak and the french fries, he licked the plate. Then he licked the plate again. Then he licked his lips and lay on the floor by Tim's feet. He half-closed his eyes and drifted into a quiet sleep. At that moment, Grk was the happiest dog in the world.